Congratulations!

When you opened this book, you took your first step toward understanding your jealousy and how it works. The rest of the journey will show you how to make it work *for* you.

Consult THE JEALOUSY DIAGNOSTIC INDEX to help you sort out just how strong a grip the monster has on you. Examine THE JEALOUSY FOLLIES and SLEUTHING, and they'll prove you're not alone—no matter how crazy you think your behavior might be.

Make use of THE JEALOUSY FIRST-AID KIT. It's just what it says it is: a few simple procedures to help you get free when the monster's got you in a stranglehold.

Jealousy is a signal. Once you know the code you can make your life better than you ever hoped it could be!

JEALOUSY

Eugene Schoenfeld, M.D.

PINNACLE BOOKS NEW YORK

The author wishes to thank Lora Foundation,
John Grissim, Bill Levy, William Robbins, and Jerry Rubin
for their help.

JEALOUSY: TAMING THE GREEN-EYED MONSTER

Copyright © 1979 by Eugene Schoenfeld

A Pinnacle Books edition, published by special arrangement with
Holt, Rinehart and Winston.

Holt, Rinehart and Winston edition/January 1980

Pinnacle edition/December 1984

ISBN: 0-523-42123-0

Can. ISBN: 0-523-43097-3

Cover art by Paul Stinson

Printed in the United States of America

PINNACLE BOOKS, INC.
1430 Broadway
New York, New York 10018

9 8 7 6 5 4 3 2 1

TO BARBARA AND IRINA

Contents

JEALOUSY

1   A New Taboo

You know the feeling. You know it and you hate it. You feel threatened, afraid, helpless, angry, insecure, betrayed— emotions all mixed up somehow with love. And when you've got it you can't think of anything else.

Depending on how you feel at the time, the most insignificant events can trigger it: a phone call taken in the other room, the "can we make it another time" reply, or perhaps the chance encounter when you found your partner engrossed in an intense conversation, a conversation that seemed to change course when you appeared. Did it really? It doesn't matter.

Regardless of the circumstances, chances are you weren't anticipating your reaction. It happens fast—some old wound opens deep inside. Maybe you recognize it for what it is—jealousy.

I first began thinking seriously about jealousy several years ago at the end of a long affair with a warm, loving woman I'll call Judith. For most of the time we were together, I never doubted she wanted to be with anyone but me. I was always saying no, no, no to her yes, yes, yes. Only twice was I jealous because of her, though I'm sorry to say I made her jealous many times.

The first time I felt jealous of Judith we were in New York at a party on a Staten Island houseboat. She was pretty and vivacious, with an openness that caused people to like her immediately. As we prepared to leave the party, she gave her name and address to a man who shortly planned to visit the West Coast, where we lived. I didn't like that at all. Even though we lived separately (against her wishes), and I saw other women, I felt she was *mine*. I also felt a dent in my pride. What would people think of me if she invited other men to call on her?

I wasn't prepared to make the kind of commitment Judith wanted, and she, quite rightly, thought it time to move in together or go our separate ways.

But one night she was supposed to be at my house while a visiting girl friend stayed in her apartment. It wasn't until dawn that she slipped into bed and went to sleep. When we were both awake later that morning she confessed she'd made love with someone else the night before. Judith was trying to make me jealous, and she certainly succeeded. I'd just finished a shower and remember furiously drying myself with a towel while loudly denouncing her infidelity. She was shocked at my shouting because I'd never really raised my voice to her before in anger. I recall my surprise at recognizing that, despite being so upset, it felt good to feel something so strongly. My emotions had been on an even keel so long it was a relief to bellow out, even in anger. It seemed that jealousy had some positive aspects, too.

I was writing a weekly newspaper column at the time and noticed a growing number of letters from readers asking advice on how to reduce or eliminate jealousy, particularly sexual jealousy. The same topic seemed to turn up more and more frequently in conversations with friends and associates. I found also, during talks at colleges or to community organizations, that if the subject of jealousy was mentioned, even in passing, it almost invariably became the exclusive subject of the question-and-answer period that followed. Many people found it more difficult to discuss openly their jealousy than their sex lives. Some felt guilty and regarded the emotion as immature, invalid, and contrary to modern, liberated lifestyles. I had few answers to their questions about jealousy.

A few years after my relationship with Judith ended, I became involved with Jeannie, a beautiful, funny, altogether wonderful woman who worked in television. We met during an interview and found in each other qualities we admired, respected, wanted, and felt we needed. We fell in love. There were only two problems. We lived in different cities, and she was married. From the beginning Jeannie assured me she had an "open" marriage. In fact, she said she and her husband lived together only because of their children and financial obligations, that each of them pursued a completely separate social life. I visited their house often and her husband did seem quite friendly and open. The three of us even went sailing together. But all along I told her I could not imagine myself in his position; that I would not, could not, be so magnanimous.

Jeannie and I once went to the Bahamas for ten days. I flew to New York and waited for her at the airport, as we'd arranged. She arrived with her husband, who had driven her to the airport, and, since the flight was delayed, we all three had breakfast together. Afterward, he waved a cheerful good-bye as we flew off on our holiday. At the time I could not understand his cavalier attitude. As it turned out, he was just trying to make the best of a difficult situation. He wanted to keep her at any cost, even if it meant the torment of trying to suppress his deeply felt emotions. But she was determined to end their marriage and later did.

Jeannie and I planned radio and television shows, articles and books, including this one. But jealousy prevented us from working together and ultimately was an important factor in ending our relationship. People would sometimes recognize me at public functions, and she felt threatened by the attention I received from other women. Not that I was at all immune to the emotion. The more I wanted her, the more intense my emotions, the more susceptible I became to feelings of jealousy.

Conversations with friends convinced me my feelings were widely shared. Most people I knew wanted both close and varied relationships. They wished to retain shared intimacy yet believed their lives could be enriched by knowing a variety of other people. Despite experience and reason, jealousy disrupted not only their plans but also their relationships. By now, I knew an explanation of jealousy and some solutions were urgently needed—by me, if no one else! It seemed to me that creatures ingenious enough to transmit their voices, images, and even bodies through space should be able to deal better with an emotion that so often blocks human communication.

My study began with intensive library research, which revealed a concern with jealousy through the ages. Some useful observations were found in sources as diverse as the Bible, Darwin, and Freud. But surprisingly few books were wholly devoted to the subject.

Turning to the many available books on human relationships, I found that, while they contained valuable advice on how to live, love, relate, and fight fair, they failed to offer much useful advice about jealousy.

After the library research was concluded, over a hundred men and women of all ages were interviewed—husbands wives, singles, and couples—people with widely varied lifestyles, educational backgrounds, sexual preferences, and occupations.

I obtained the interviews in the following way. First, I defined certain categories such as single, married, gay, communal, swingers, old, and young. Next, I drew up a list of individuals within these categories I thought might have insights into jealousy. As it turned out, *everyone* had insights into jealousy, since this forceful emotion is part of being human. If you discuss jealousy with others, you'll find the same reactions I've heard described over and over—fear, grief, loneliness, anger. Sometimes the responses are savage, like many of those reported here.

In sum, then, this book is based on interviews, research, and my own experiences.

Jealousy is not envy. They differ not only in the relationships involved but in the intensity of the feelings they cause. Envy usually concerns a relationship between two people, jealousy three or more people. Envy is usually about things rather than people, but not always. You might be envious of a neighbor's house or job. You might envy an acquaintance because his companion makes charming conversation. He might envy you because your wife or husband makes a lot of money. You might envy a friend, her good looks, charisma, or apparently well-behaved children. She might envy you your lack of children. Envy is somehow more passive than jealousy, wistful rather than grief-stricken, more pique than anger.

Jealousy and envy are both unpleasant, but envy is like getting stung by a mosquito or, at worst, a bee. It hurts but it's not overwhelming. Jealousy can be like having a rusty jagged knife stuck in your gut and—depending on the circumstances—slowly twisted. You rarely hear of people killing because of envy.

The components of jealousy are fear or anticipated grief, a loss of self-worth, a stirring of early feelings of insecurity, and anger directed at a loved one or whoever is diverting his or her attention. Usually one or two of these components are felt more than the others.

From the beginning, jealousy has had a bad press. The Song of Solomon tells us, "Jealousy is as cruel as the grave." There are various types of jealousy—sibling jealousy, professional jealousy, and social jealousy, to name a few—but sexual jealousy is the one that affects most people most often, and seems to hurt worst. Asked what jealousy meant to her, an attorney said, "It basically boils down to two things with me. One, I'm feeling left out and I want to get involved with someone else. I want the sexual interchange that they're having. Or I want to have that person close so I feel like I'm not losing him. It's a fear of loss and a fear of being left out."

Although almost all humans have felt this complex emotion, some people experience it more often or more profoundly than others. And some people seem to cause much more jealousy than they experience.

A beautiful Los Angeles actress wryly described a jealousy episode this way: "I was infatuated with a man who seemed to be extremely busy. After a while I started getting suspicious because he was away so much. He was Chinese and sometimes I'd tell myself he had mysterious business in Chinatown. He said he had to travel a lot . . . but somehow something didn't seem right. I started looking for clues, reading crumpled notes and labels in his wastebaskets. I even began following him and lost several jobs because I had to include following him around in my day's plans." She turned beet red and laughed, "My God, I even staked out his house! I would park at night on a nearby hill and watch his windows. Once I saw him in a window without a shirt and just freaked out.

"Finally I saw *her* but I couldn't stop. One day I confronted them as they left his house. He was supposed to be in San Francisco. When he saw me he turned pale and said, 'I'll explain everything.' Even then I wanted to believe him."

Tracking a loved one is surprisingly common among the jealous. I found this sleuthing phenomenon so intriguing you'll find a whole chapter devoted to the subject.

Not everyone believes it's useful or necessary to do away with or even modify jealous feelings. Some cogent arguments for jealousy as a protective device can be made. A bookstore owner remarked, "Jealousy helps control the population." And he was only half-joking.

A recent newspaper article quoted actor Michael Landon and his wife as saying jealousy keeps their marriage together. Lynn Landon said she felt that most women wouldn't like a husband who's so jealous that he couldn't let his wife out of his sight, and most men wouldn't put up with a wife who thought every attractive woman was after him.

Michael added that jealousy worked for them. It kept their marriage strong because it didn't allow them to take one another for granted. It kept them on their toes. It's a constant reminder that after all these years they still found each other so attractive they each thought everybody else wanted what they had.

They're not the only people who use jealousy to validate love for their partners. The pain, the rage, the despair seem to say to some people, "See how much I care? I wouldn't feel these things if I didn't love you."

Some spiritual teachers say jealousy exists to be overcome; it's an indicator of the pain that accompanies selfish possession. As we become less possessive and self-centered, we should feel less jealousy. And jealousy is viewed by others as a trigger for growth, an incentive to overcome areas of emotional vulnerability.

* * *

Human beings can verbalize their thoughts, describe their passions. Since animals cannot, we don't know with complete certainty that they experience jealousy. But anyone with a pet dog or cat has observed unusual behavior that could be interpreted as jealousy. When my own dog, Ahab, a sensitive, gentle Great Dane, felt I was paying too much attention to another animal or even to another person, he would often stick his head between us as if to ask for attention and petting. If animals are jealous, then we may be speaking of an instinct, an instinct perhaps retained by human beings.

Instinctual behavior has protective functions. How could the painfully primitive feelings caused by jealousy be useful? Until recent concerns about overpopulation and challenges to social systems arose, preservation of the family was acknowledged as essential to the continuation of the human race. A threat to the family from within or without was a threat to life itself, individually and collectively. Taking a club to a rival's skull might keep a cavemate closer to life-essential duties of home and hearth. Jealousy may be a vestigial but still powerful remnant of the territorial imperative. In many ways jealousy is analogous to (or even part of) the basic fight-or-flight mechanism. We may feel like punching out our rival or retreating to morbid emotional corners, but neither response is socially useful today. That's why it seems that handling jealousy better is a step forward in human relationships.

We have many opportunities for social intercourse and other intimacies, but are torn by seemingly opposite desires—wanting more human contact, but feeling jealous when those we value want the same contact. We can leap sexual barriers with a single bound, but get snagged painfully on the horns of the green-eyed monster.

Jealousy has always been with us, but the social changes

of recent years have added something new. Besides the unpleasant feelings jealousy causes, the emotion itself is now treated as an embarrassment. A few years ago sexuality was rarely admitted to or even discussed in open conversation. Now we almost all feel sexuality is normal, healthy, even a human right.

But expressing or even admitting to jealousy is regarded in many circles today as socially unacceptable, boorish, uncool. "I can't waste my time with people who are jealous" is a frequent response among people who feel they're socially mobile. Apart from people who live in experimental setups like communes and group marriages, many wish to enlarge their social circles, be more open, liberated. Even among people who freely admit to being jealous, there's a belief that jealousy is an immature emotion, something to be outgrown, a feeling unworthy of intelligent, sophisticated, socially aware individuals. But the bastard won't go away. Not by wishing, anyway. The rise of open relationships and women's liberation have made significant numbers of people aware that we don't possess one another. And it's true, of course. But realizing something intellectually is not equivalent to feeling it. We may believe ideally that the world would be a better place without jealousy. We may even believe we do not have the right to be jealous of another. But belief is not sufficient. Just ask your friends about jealousy and what it means to them. The beast is still with us, and its effects are worse than ever before. The feelings it causes are bad enough, and always were, but now we're not even supposed to have those feelings. Shame or guilt over jealousy is added to the discomfort of the jealous feelings themselves. A basic emotion is now taboo.

Susceptibility to jealousy is somewhat similar to susceptibility to infectious disease. It depends upon your general status. If you're overly fatigued or overly worried, you're more likely to catch a cold than you ordinarily would be. Similarly, you're less likely to be jealous at times when you feel good, when your work is going well, when your body feels strong.

Jealousy cannot be separated from other parts of your life. The more insecure you feel, for instance, the more likely you are to be jealous. And if you become more basically secure, chances are you will be less jealous. At first, this realization may make it seem as if singling out jealousy is hopeless, since it's part of a complex life situation. But it's not hopeless. In fact, you can work on jealousy itself and produce beneficial changes not only in this specific area, but in other components of your personality. Because jealousy can be so important a part of the way you relate to the world, reducing its negative effects is a most useful way to improve general emotional well-being. By successfully coping with jealousy, you can make yourself stronger in many other ways. If you like, look at jealousy as a handle, an opening to your personality.

When jealousy arises, there are better ways of dealing with it than withdrawing and sulking or lashing out in anger. The key to dealing with jealousy more effectively is understanding what it is, what it isn't, where it comes from, and how to prevent it. When we're in the grip of jealous feelings they're almost impossible to ignore *because they were designed to capture our full attention*. That's why prevention here, as in all areas of mind-body health, is more productive than treating the injury.

In the following chapters we will examine jealousy and how it affects a variety of individuals, some like you, some very different. We will then discuss useful ways to eliminate jealousy as a destructive factor in your life or in the lives of those you care for.

Jealousy may or may not be an outmoded emotion. But there's no doubt jealousy is a new taboo and that you can learn to deal with it more effectively.

2 The Jealousy Diagnostic Index

The Jealousy Diagnostic Index is a series of questions designed to help you locate areas of vulnerability to jealousy. Before you read any further, find out your own capacity for jealousy. Answer these questions, based on the way you would probably feel in the given situation, rather than the way you would prefer to feel. Next, take the test from the viewpoint of your partner. Then, when you have read the rest of the book, take the test again and compare your scores. What did you learn about jealousy—and yourself?

Every normal person is susceptible to jealousy given the right—or wrong—circumstances. These situations involve factors that influence one's sense of self-esteem, like physical well-being and work satisfaction, as well as intrinsic feelings of self-worth. How do you feel when a loved one pays undue attention to something or someone else? Is it really undue attention or are you unduly sensitive? Are you always oversensitive or only in a specific limited life situation?

The questions are designed to help you deal with a difficult issue by outlining problem areas. When choosing answers to these questions, you may find yourself thinking, "Well, that depends." But pick the answer most closely corresponding to the way you would feel and respond to the situation described. You may want to jot down the answers on a separate piece of paper. There is no "pass" or "fail" score.

PART 1

Answer TRUE or FALSE:

1. Everyone knows what jealousy feels like.   T F
2. Sometimes you get so jealous you can't eat.   T F
3. Sometimes when you feel jealous, you go on T F
   eating binges.
4. At parties you are aware of every move and T F
   gesture when your partner talks to someone
   else.
5. Jealousy is a major problem in your life.   T F
6. You are more jealous than most people you T F
   know.
7. You should have outgrown jealousy long ago.   T F
8. Often you are jealous of your partner's friends, T F
   even when you know they are not lovers.
9. Thinking or hearing about your partner's former T F
   lovers makes you jealous.
10. Sometimes you seem to like feeling jealous.   T F
11. Sometimes you like making other people jealous.   T F
12. You often like making other people feel jealous.   T F
13. Sometimes you cause jealousy when you don't T F
    mean to.
14. You often seem to cause jealousy when you don't T F
    mean to.

15. Jealousy is no longer part of your life.   T F
16. You don't care if your partner flirts with T F
    others.
17. More than once you have hit a lover or rival T F
    because of jealousy.
18. More than once you have threatened to hit a T F
    lover or rival because of jealousy.
19. More than once you have thought of hitting T F
    a lover or rival because of jealousy.
20. People seem to go out of their way to make T F
    you jealous.
21. You have followed or otherwise spied on some- T F
    one because of jealousy.
22. Not much time passes between your encounters T F
    with jealousy.
23. You are usually successful at controlling your T F
    jealous feelings.
24. You often fly into a jealous rage.   T F
25. When you're jealous, it's hard to admit it to T F
    others.
26. At social functions like parties you tend to stay T F
    very close to your partner to fend off possible
    rivals.
27. You must know where your partner is at all T F
    times.
28. You have fantasized about taking revenge on a T F
    rival.
29. You have taken revenge on a rival.   T F
30. Jealousy has caused you to consider hiring a T F
    private detective.
31. You tell people you're not the jealous type, T F
    even though you may be very jealous indeed.
32. You avoid close relationships because such T F
    situations can lead to jealousy.

33. It would be a major crisis if you discovered your   T F
    partner had had a casual sexual encounter with
    someone else.

34. It would be a major crisis if you discovered your   T F
    partner had a continuing, though casual, sexual
    relationship.

35. You find it hard to accept criticism.   T F

36. You are generally pretty lonely.   T F

PART 2

The following questions have multiple-choice answers.
Choose the one that most closely represents your attitude
or the way you might respond to the given situation.

1. A person with whom you're nonexclusively involved receives a telephone call while the two of you are
watching TV. Judging from the conversation and tone of
voice, the caller is also involved with your partner. The
conversation lasts a friendly five minutes. You would feel:

a. Unconcerned
b. Mildly irritated
c. Offended and resentful
d. Really angry

2. In the preceding situation, you would:

a. Dismiss the episode as unimportant
b. Ask who the caller was, though you're not jealous
c. Ask who the caller was because you're feeling jealous
d. Hide your feelings and hope they'll pass in a while
e. Tell your partner the caller should have been asked to
   call back at another time
f. Get up and leave the house

3. You've just returned from a week-long business trip. You and your live-in partner pay a visit to a mutual friend next door. At one point your neighbor is looking for an appointment book. "Isn't it in the top drawer of your bedroom dresser?" your partner asks helpfully. You would:

a. Think nothing of the remark
b. Suspect some hanky-panky
c. Suspect hanky-panky and be jealous
d. Consider other reasons for your partner's remark

4. In these circumstances, you would:

a. Say nothing
b. Do nothing for the time being, but be watchful
c. Ask for an explanation when you're alone with your partner if the matter concerns you
d. Confront both of them right then and get to the bottom of it

5. You learn your supposedly monogamous partner has another lover. You would feel:

a. Annoyed
b. Relieved
c. Somewhat jealous
d. Betrayed, angry, and hurt

6. Accordingly, you would:

a. Say nothing, hide your feelings
b. Do nothing as long as your partner continues to give you the same amount of warmth and affection
c. Confront your partner, express your feelings, and work through the crisis
d. Plan your revenge
e. Find another lover for yourself

7. You are invited to an important dinner party where a serious rival for your partner will also be a guest. You would feel:

a. No jealousy
b. A little jealous
c. Jealous and jittery
d. Very jealous—enraged, fear-stricken

8. You would then:

a. Accept the invitation; the guest list gives you no problem
b. Discuss your feelings with your partner before accepting the invitation
c. Accept the invitation, then discuss your feelings with your partner
d. Decline the invitation without admitting the reason
e. Declare your feelings and decline the invitation

9. You accepted the invitation. On the way home your partner is bubbling with happiness. You would feel:

a. Curious
b. Pleased your partner had a good time
c. A little jealous for a little while
d. Very jealous and angry
e. Like punching out your partner or the other person

10. Once home, your partner wants to make love. You feel jealous. You would:

a. Make love, if you felt like it
b. Hide your jealous feelings and make love
c. Invent a "headache" type excuse
d. Vent your feelings and declare you don't want to make love

e. Vent your feelings, then see what happens
f. Make passionate love to get your partner very interested in you

11. Since arriving at another party, your partner has been totally engrossed in conversation with someone else. You would:

a. Be unconcerned
b. Ignore the situation for now, but discuss it later when the two of you are alone
c. Take your partner aside and calmly express your feelings
d. Tell your partner you're leaving unless more attention is paid to you
e. Leave the party and drive home alone
f. Leave the party with a different partner

12. Your partner is quite vulnerable to jealousy but at the moment is openly flirting with someone else. You feel jealous. You would:

a. Try to ignore the situation
b. Take your partner aside privately and explain how you feel
c. Do nothing until the party is over, then discuss your feelings
d. Tell your partner right now to stop flirting
e. Find someone you can flirt with too

13. You discover your partner is involved in a homosexual relationship. You would feel:

a. No jealousy
b. Jealous, but less so than if it was a heterosexual relationship

c. More jealous than if it was a heterosexual relationship
d. Equally jealous regardless of the rival's sex
e. Perplexed

14. You have a close relationship with someone, but both of you have sex with others and know it. The proper time interval your partner should observe between sex with others and with you is:

a. The time interval doesn't matter
b. The time interval doesn't matter as long as you don't know about it
c. A week or more
d. Several days
e. One day
f. A few hours with a shower and/or douche
g. One hour with a Boraxo-soap shower and/or industrial-strength douche

3 The Jealousy Follies

As I've indicated earlier, a major reason for researching and writing this book was to understand and better control my own jealousy. But the cure didn't happen right away. Far from it. Sometimes I even wondered whether the necessary preoccupation with the subject only made me more prone to jealousy.

While planning and outlining this book, I was seeing a well-known feminist author. She was looking for a literary agent at the time, and one of her friends arranged a meeting with a newly successful agent visiting from New York. The three of us had dinner together, and throughout the evening I was aware of the agent trying to charm my woman friend. Of course he was! He wanted her as a client. But I was at loose ends at the time and particularly vulnerable to jealousy. The following afternoon my friend and I were sunbathing on her balcony and discussing tentative plans for the evening. We'd been invited to a party, but she was strangely vague and suggested I might like going alone. Just then her telephone rang. She answered it, then pointedly took the telephone inside the house, where she finished her conversation. It was the New York agent.

Even though, as it turned out, my friend met him for only a few hours in the late afternoon, I was seized by jealousy. I was angry, felt threatened, probably sulked. True, she had been indelicate about taking the phone inside. Preventing jealousy in people around you is just as important as coping with your own jealousy. But there was little reason for me to feel as I did. Although both the agent and my friend may have sized each other up sexually, as people do on first meetings, socializing was only their means to discuss business. As the agent later told me, "To me she was just a big paperback book." But to me she was a big lovely lover secretively giving her attentions to someone else. Though the intensity of my feelings seemed out of proportion when compared with the provocation, I didn't know how to cope at the time, except badly.

But I took solace, as I worked on the book, from some of the stories that I unearthed. Because taboos are not discussed, victims of jealousy often feel they are alone in their troubles, and this was certainly the case with me. It was a relief to come across cases of jealousy much more severe than mine. Also, I thought I could recognize similarities in these tales to those of people I know. In any case, I took comfort in the knowledge that jealousy commonly overpowers logic and reasoned behavior. And I discovered that there are ways to deal with it constructively.

Harry Stack Sullivan was a psychiatrist who broke away from traditional psychoanalysis and founded a school of thought based on interpersonal relations. He died relatively young and his teachings are preserved only because some of his lectures were recorded and transcribed. In one of the books posthumously assembled from his talks he says:

> Jealousy is, I think, in some ways even less welcome than anxiety; and when I say that, I am not engaging in hyperbole, because anxiety, if at all severe, is *utterly* unwelcome. But jealousy, in my experience with people who really suffer it, seems to come very close to providing an adequate picture of the now old-fashioned Christian hell.

Did Dr. Sullivan also suffer severely from jealousy? Remember that the above words were spoken, not written. Perhaps he started to say, "But jealousy, in my experience," only to catch himself and add "with people who really suffer it." From the rhythm of his words, I would guess Harry Stack Sullivan struggled with jealousy. Admitting to it isn't easy, particularly for those in the helping professions. But recognizing these feelings is the first step to dealing with them more effectively.

While doing a radio program I invited listeners to send me their thoughts on jealousy. A twenty-one-year-old woman wrote:

> Jealousy is a painful disease. It nags at your head. It makes you dream terrible things, and makes you think of things unbelievable. When I get jealous I go off into an unknown world of hate. I think of sickening things to do to people. My heart beats fast and blood seems to rush to my head. My face burns with heat. I can't hold my temper, though I try very hard to hold it in. I went through stages where I hated my boyfriend so much I could kill him. I'm not really sure, but I feel my mind would be at ease if he were dead. I feel that I could accept this fact. But seeing him with other women and trying to keep cool is something

unbelievable to bear. This pain is lingering on and on, and it lives within at all times. To me it is a disease, and I wish I knew what to do about it.

Anger, despair, competitiveness, rejection, and betrayal often combine to create a powerful desire to lash out, to seek revenge. The pounding heart, flushed skin, thoughts of violence, and feelings of hatred this woman is experiencing are commonly felt by people in the throes of jealousy. But most of us don't act on these impulses, don't carry out vengeful fantasies. The peaks and piques of jealousy are usually short-lived, allowing us to maintain self-control. Unfortunately all too many people are psychologically strung tight. When they are stressed beyond their limits we may read about them in the daily press. The following seven tales of passion and rage were obtained from newspaper files.

In rural England a forty-nine-year-old man's wife had taken up with another man. Her jilted husband hung a battery detonator around his neck, stuffed explosives under his coat, and hunted down his wife's lover. When he found him he pressed the button. The explosion that followed produced tremendous damage but somehow left both men alive. The husband staggered to his wounded victim and battered him to death with the battery box. "My only regret," he told police, "is that I too am not dead."

Another item from the British press tells of a jealous Englishwoman's thwarted suicide attempt. Believing her absent husband was cheating on her, the grief-stricken woman hurled herself from the balcony of their sixth-floor apartment. Her fall was broken by her husband, just entering the building. He died, she lived.

*   *   *

A jealous quarrel between a distraught man and his
former wife in a Texas community resulted in his arrest for
drunken driving, assault with a deadly weapon, vandalism,
and resisting arrest. According to police, the woman had
just returned home and parked her 1974 Plymouth when
she saw her ex-husband approach from the rear in his Ford
pickup. She fled the car as he accelerated his truck to a
high rate of speed, ramming the Plymouth. The woman's
sixteen-year-old daughter had stationed herself behind the
car to keep it from being rammed, but had to jump out of
the way. Several crashes later the Plymouth was on the
median strip of the street. The man then backed up to the
northwest corner of the intersection, floored his accelerator,
and rammed the car onto the opposite sidewalk, through
thirty feet of fence, across a backyard, and into a swimming
pool. The pickup also plunged into the pool.

Most newspaper stories involving jealousy are far grimmer.
There is the case of Edward Alloway, a thirty-seven-year-
old custodian for the California State University at Fullerton.
People who knew Alloway regarded him as good-looking
and quiet, "a typical nice guy, someone you'd say 'Hi!' to
always." His public image changed drastically during five
minutes of terror in the summer of 1976, inside the campus library building where he worked. Alloway was de-
spondent over the breakup of his three-year marriage and
extremely jealous of his wife, whom co-workers described
as "a sweet, trusting, naive woman-child." Even during
happier times he was considered jealous of everybody—
"even her family, he was that type of boy." "He didn't
like his job," a friend said. "His marriage was breaking
up."

   The news reports didn't indicate exactly what caused
Alloway's mind to snap the day he entered the campus

library's ultramodern Instructional Media Center with a new semiautomatic .22 caliber rifle and began methodically shooting those present. After leaving three dead and one mortally wounded, Alloway ran into a hallway to reload. According to the *Los Angeles Times* story, as he ran back through the building, witnesses overheard him muttering "I'm going to kill all those sons of bitches for fucking my wife." More shooting followed. By the time he fled the building, Alloway left seven university employees dead and two wounded. He was arrested at the Hilton Inn in nearby Anaheim while visiting his estranged wife, a banquet waitress. "It was over with when he came here. He was a little boy again," her employer reported.

SURGEONS REATTACH SEVERED MALE ORGAN read the headline of an Associated Press story out of Atlanta on October 10, 1977. A drunk twenty-four-year-old laborer and his eighteen-year-old half-brother raided the apartment of a twenty-year-old student who was dating the laborer's estranged wife. While the younger brother held a gun on the student's roommate, the laborer choked the student unconscious, tied his hands and feet, and cut off his penis with a butcher knife.

The laborer later pleaded guilty to multiple charges and was sentenced to life imprisonment plus forty-five years. The student was taken to his university infirmary, then to another hospital before being transferred to Emory University Hospital in Atlanta. There a team of plastic surgeons and neurologists reattached the severed penis.

Jealous revenge apparently takes this concrete form all too often. Severed penises were successfully reattached in 1976 at Nare Medical University in Japan and Massachusetts General Hospital in Boston, and at a Trenton, New Jersey, hospital in 1977.

* * *

It would be difficult to imagine a more cruel example of jealousy-induced killing than the 1962 case of Dr. Gaza de Kaplany and his bride Hajna. Dr. de Kaplany, a San Francisco anesthesiologist, became convinced his young and beautiful wife had taken a lover and was ready at any moment to leave him. But he hid his feelings of jealousy and rejection. One night he seized his bride, stripped her naked, and tied her down. He then began torturing her by applying nitric acid to the most sensitive parts of her body. Many hours later the woman was rushed to a hospital, where she remained in critical condition for thirty-four days before dying.

"During the trial," recalls a lawyer whose firm later represented de Kaplany, "we used the Jekyll and Hyde concept as our argument for the defense. There was the de Kaplany who was the loving husband and the 'other' de Kaplany, the pathologically jealous lover, jealous of his wife, jealous of her beauty, and deathly afraid she would leave him."

For the acid bath torture slaying of his wife, Dr. de Kaplany was convicted of first-degree murder, but his life was spared. After serving twelve years in state prisons, he was quietly paroled and now works with a Seventh-Day Adventist medical group on Taiwan.

If you think you are extremely jealous or know someone else who is very jealous, and are feeling uneasy at this point, relax for a moment. The cases presented are very much out of the ordinary—that's why I selected them. You or the person you're concerned about isn't likely to go on a murderous rampage even when "jealous of everybody." Most chronically jealous people torture themselves, not others. They suffer severe pain, which can and should be avoided. Mastering unreasonable jealousy begins by recognizing it, in others as well as in yourself.

Judging from my interviews, your own circle of friends and acquaintances probably contains tales of jealousy as bizarre as—if less violent than—those found in newspapers, though I do know someone who served time for killing his wife's lover. Everyone has experienced at least one jealous episode of general interest, if only in terms of strong feelings. Some of the best conversations, adventures, and relationships I've had began by asking people about their jealousy. Try it yourself. Ask the next person you care to speak with to describe a personal exerience involving jealousy—unless you're likely to be part of the story. Save *those* tales for later.

When you discuss jealousy with people you know or want to know, as I did, you may hear stories like these:

"I had just returned home from London and was very anxious to see the woman who caused me to go abroad for a year," explained a talented novelist and screenwriter, who for several years had sworn off his other nemesis, alcohol. He squeezed some lemon juice into a glass of Calso water and continued. "When I arrived unannounced, I saw a motorcycle chained to the wrought-iron stairs outside her flat. I flew into a jealous rage. I ran up the stairs prepared to beat hell out of her and whoever was with her. It was only as I was breaking down the door that it occurred to me the motorcycle was a very large, mean-looking Harley chopper, and that the person who owned it would very likely also be very large and mean. Too late! I discovered I'd disturbed the peace of my ex-girl friend and a Hell's Angel. Thirty seconds later I found myself at the bottom of the stairs with a black eye and multiple abrasions. She stopped him from killing me."

Car revenge is a common theme in stories of jealous rage. When a young Mexican-American hospital switchboard operator learned of my research, she told me she'd just wrecked two automobiles in a jealous rage.

She rammed her boyfriend's old car broadside with her own late-model car, causing $500 damage to his auto and $400 damage to hers. She had taken action immediately after learning her boyfriend had another girl friend who was about to have his baby.

Personally, I have known a wide range of reactions resulting from jealousy. While in college, I had a date with a young woman who was also seeing a graduate student from Turkey, a jealous Turk as it developed. As we left the dormitory her other friend jumped from the shadows, grabbed me by the front of my sweater, and demanded to know where we were going. That night I learned the limit of my nonviolence—it was the sound of my new cardigan ripping. I became furious and started pummeling my rival. He screamed that I was attacking him, and we were soon pulled apart by bystanders. At first my sole regret was that I could land only body blows because he continued to cling to my clothing. He wasn't seriously injured, but my fists were sore for days afterward.

A twenty-eight-year-old woman I'll call Lynn was involved with a man who sometimes liked a ménage à trois. So did Lynn, but only when the situation didn't threaten her. Several times they had been together with a woman in her mid-thirties he'd known and loved for years. Because the older woman lived three thousand miles away, Lynn didn't feel threatened. But one night the male friend put her together with another quite attractive woman of thirty-seven who lived in the same city. Lynn thought he was paying more attention to the other woman than to her, and he may have been. Lynn had small, well-formed breasts; the older woman had large, well-formed breasts. "I didn't

like it when he put one of those big boobs in my face,"
Lynn reported. She left the bedroom, stewed around awhile
in the living room, and when she returned, found her male
friend and his new girl friend sleeping in each other's
arms. She awoke him by slapping his face smartly. Yet
Lynn still couldn't admit her true feelings. "I wasn't
jealous when I hit him," she maintained, "I just didn't
like her."

Lynn said jealousy was a major problem for her only
when she felt seriously involved in a relationship, then it
was indeed a difficult problem. Yet she believed monogamy
was impractical. Her solution? Affairs with others were
acceptable as long as they occurred in distant cities. If her
man spent the great majority of his free time with her and
rivals were geographically distant, and therefore relatively
inaccessible, her jealousy was under control. She was also
little bothered by the "zipless fuck" type of brief,
anonymous sexual encounter described by author Erica
Jong.

Few experiences can equal the embarrassment of discovering jealousy has been unleashed by a suspect who
doesn't even exist.

A building contractor I know was exceedingly jealous of
the male professional contacts of his wife, who managed
musical groups. Despite her efforts to convince him of her
innocence and disinterest in other men, he remained
suspicious. One morning after she finished a telephone
call, he exploded: "All right, goddammit! You're gonna
tell me right now just who the hell this guy Art is! You've
been talking about him on the phone all week!"

"Art who?" she replied heatedly. "I don't know any
Art."

"You sure as hell do!" he yelled. "Art Nevey or Art
Nova . . ."

"Sit down, John," she said, "you're gonna like this."
She glared angrily at him for a second before sneering:
"It's art *nouveau,* you idiot!"

Their marriage soon ended.

Discovering that one's rival in love doesn't exist is
embarrassing, but there are situations even more humiliating.
Consider the story of a woman friend who frequently
writes for *Cosmopolitan* magazine. One afternoon in my
office she told me:

"For some time I've had a steady relationship with a
man who left his wife for me, and yet he hasn't wanted us
to live together. He spends some time with his estranged
wife, but that doesn't make me jealous. . . . I'm jealous of
his dog!

"There are moments when he's giving affection to his
dog, where he hugs her and tells her how adorable she is,
and kisses her . . . it's not just a pat on the head, 'Good
old Fido'—it's this rush of enthusiasm.

"I have nothing against the dog, but if anyone feels
overcome with affection, I figure that I'm a more appropriate
subject—given a choice between me and the dog. I mean
when I'm not around, then he can just go gaga over the
dog. I don't want him doing it when I'm around. I guess
part of it stems from my feelings about dogs, particularly
about my own dog, Sonny. I've had Sonny for six years
and occasionally I get these kind of me-and-my-dog
feelings—that I don't need any man. And I project the
same feelings onto my man friend. I guess there's a slight
fear that suddenly one day he'll say 'to hell with all these
women' and go off with his dog."

The target of jealous rage may be completely innocent.
While on duty in an emergency room, I treated a man who
was a victim of the pent-up anger of his wife's former

husband. The two men had never been rivals. In fact, the wife hadn't met her second husband until long after she'd divorced the first. Nonetheless, when the wife and her new husband went to her ex-husband's house to pick up her visiting children, a violent argument ensued.

The ex-husband pulled out a pistol and began shouting while waving it in the air. Husband number two, a big burly type, grabbed husband number one, pushed him outside and slammed the door. The ex-husband fired accurately through the door, striking the second man in the groin.

On examining the bullet's entry wound, I found something peculiar—a large piece of white plastic. X-rays of the man's pelvis showed smaller fragments of opaque material in a line leading to an intact bullet. The man's left trouser pocket contained a shattered disposable white cigarette lighter, which had apparently deflected the bullet away from vital and precious organs. I could feel a small lump just beneath the skin of the patient's left buttock. By making a small incision, I was able to grasp and remove the bullet with a pair of forceps. I'd hoped to keep the bullet as a souvenir, but the police seized it as evidence.

I've briefly described my affair with Jeannie, the married woman whose husband pretended not to care. She subsequently became involved with a well-known magazine editor. "Well," she told me when we were once more loving, if not lovers, "at least he doesn't make me jealous like you did." But he soon became very jealous of *her*. She is an attractive media personality whose work requires frequent travel within the metropolitan area where her programs originate. Her editor friend became more and more suspicious as their relationship developed. He grew curious about her movements and one evening was observed checking her automobile's odometer to verify she'd driven only from their home to the broadcast studio. Finally, one Christmas, she was stunned by his gift suggestion—a radio paging device worn on her belt so he could contact her wherever she was at any time.

"Can you imagine?" she laughed. "There'd I'd be in the middle of whatever when suddenly: *beep-beep-beep*. A gift like that could ruin me sexually." She found a tactful way to refuse the radio beeper.

Often during the course of my research for this book, a friend would say, "You want an outrageous jealousy story? Talk to . . ." More rarely, I was referred to people thought not to be jealous. Almost always, as it developed, these "nonjealous" individuals either masked their feelings, made others jealous, or didn't become involved much with other people. But there were some people who seemed to have mastered the emotion. Not that they were completely immune to jealousy. Every normal person is susceptible to jealousy given the right—or wrong—circumstances. These socially active people, susceptible yet rarely victims of jealousy, provided valuable clues to eliminating the follies associated with the emotion.

At first I considered interviewing numerous celebrities, but soon realized they were more likely to be guarded than people whose identities would not be revealed. I was introduced to Daniel Ellsberg, for instance, and told him of this work. His response had something to do with the way political cooperation in reunited Vietnam had virtually eliminated social jealousy. He made it clear he had nothing whatever to say in print about romantic jealousy. Musician David Crosby groaned loudly when told of the project, so I mercifully dropped the subject. You will run across some celebrities here and there in this book, but only because they had some unique thoughts about the subject.

Some of the most interesting interviews developed

accidentally. Like the Saturday night I was invited to an unusual going-away party for an unusual friend.

Entering the club rented for the occasion, I noticed an attractive woman sitting on a bar stool wearing a low-cut dress. I could hardly help noticing her since the elastic top of her dress was tucked completely beneath her breasts. Luigi, a friend who makes television commercials, introduced me to his friend, Kathryn. Kathryn described herself as a "full-time student, part-time hooker." She was the daughter of a college professor. When I told her I was doing research for a book on jealousy, she asked to be interviewed. We met a week later in her apartment.

Kathryn related a story about living in Cambridge, Massachusetts, with a Harvard graduate student. They weren't getting along well, so one morning she told him she refused to have any more sex with him. She made a lengthwise crease in the bedspread and said, "We'll sleep in the same bed but that's your side and this is my side." Kathryn paced about her apartment as she continued her story.

"Well, a week later he brought someone else home. I had always told him if he ever brought another lady home I would probably just leap into bed with them because I'd always had fantasies about getting it on with a woman. But what happened was I stayed up all that night in the next room reading *The Story of O* and listening to them make love rather loudly. I wouldn't say they were being loud on purpose, but they were into it. I know *I* got into it. Actually I'd met her before and I didn't particularly like her. She was bleached blonde with an ordinary face but a fantastic body. When Jerry had introduced us he'd thrown it up to me that she was a 'nice Jewish girl' and I was a *shiksa*. In fact I was forbidden in his parents' home. I went to their house once and his father told him, 'As a courtesy to your mother would you please refrain from bringing her into the house?'

"So Jerry brought a nice Jewish girl home to our bed. The next day I had a fit. When he came home I started throwing things at him: books, cats. I picked up the kittens we had and threw them at him, which strikes me as being a little barbaric, but the kittens all walked away from it. Somehow I wanted the claws to get him. Maybe in my mind I was throwing *The Story of O*.

"We went into the kitchen together and continued shouting. At one point I was standing between him and the bathroom door and he was angry because I stood in his way. He grabbed my left breast, then pushed me down. I shouted, 'You better not sleep tonight because I'm gonna cut your balls off!' I knew he'd had heavy-duty castration dreams as a child. When he came back we were sitting in the kitchen and I jammed a butcher knife into the chair between his legs. He really jumped!

"Anyway, various things happened over the course of the next couple of hours. At one point he slapped me across the face and told me to shut up. He was wearing his college ring and it really walloped me. I got up and yelled, 'I saw stars, you creep!' He's smaller than I am." (Most people are. Kathryn is 6 feet ½ inch tall and weighs 160 pounds.) "I grabbed him by the shirt and hurled him against the wall. He came bouncing off the wall and back on top of me, throwing me back into a chair, which collapsed.

"I ended up in the hospital with a fractured ankle and a cast up to my hip. And used crutches for three months. I had a lot of time after that to think about violence and jealousy."

Most everyone has witnessed unexpected public outbursts of jealous rage. They often totally surprise the object of the fury, as well as others present. For example, Deborah, a woman in her late twenties, described a dinner party she hosted with the new man in her life:

"Gordon had invited about ten of his friends and the evening went beautifully. Until dessert. I was sitting at the opposite end of the table talking to Allen, an old friend of Gordon's. At one point Allen reached out and held my hand while we continued talking. I felt a little uncomfortable but didn't think much of it since Allen knew Gordon so well. But a few minutes later Gordon slammed his fist on the table and in a really loud voice snarled, 'Hey, why don't you give him head while you're at it?!' It shocked everybody. I ran from the table. End of dinner party. Gordon later apologized profusely."

We take you now to a large outdoor rock concert held recently in Oakland, California, a Bill Graham "Day on the Green" extravaganza.

According to friends familiar with the saga, the "wronged woman" had been furious for weeks over the attention her husband, a musician, was paying to the beguiling wife of the young rock star headlining the bill. Not only had he ignored her, he had simply disappeared for two days. Many witnesses observed the following scene: Backstage, the wife of the young rock musician was lunching at a picnic table near the troubled couple's limousine. Suddenly she spied an aristocratic woman in black approaching her with a menacing look. She leaped up from her chair, abandoned all pretense of decorum, and yelled, *"I didn't fuck him! I didn't fuck him!"*

Several friends who read these "Jealousy Follies" stories before publication have described feelings of discomfort. They said they couldn't identify with them, that these experiences were too far removed from their own. I think the opposite may be true. I think they recognized very human traits carried to extremes. It is just these extremes of feelings and action that most of us wish to prevent. And they can be prevented.

If you've ever envied the personal lives of the rich and famous, consider that neither fame nor wealth nor a combination of the two necessarily protects against jealousy. A very reliable source detailed the following story about a celebrated musician. When the event occurred he was separated from his wife. The two had parted amicably some months previously and she and their children continued to live in the couple's secluded and imposing Southern California home. One evening the musician stopped by unannounced and learned from the housekeeper that his estranged wife and her lover of some months standing were in the upstairs bedroom. He went up and knocked. No answer. He tried the door. It was locked.

There was logically no reason for him to be upset. He knew she had a love interest, although he had never met him. There was no secret revealed, no surprise, no scandal. And wasn't the house now her domain? He really had no right to barge in. He wasn't being cockolded. He was sensitive to her privacy . . . but suddenly he was jealous.

He went down to the living room, picked up a long-handled axe by the fireplace, returned to the upstairs bedroom, and began methodically smashing through the door. Shouts of protest were heard on the other side. He continued chopping. He knew he was making the room's occupants fear for their lives. He knew he wanted them to feel it. In fact, as his best songs showed, he knew a lot about love and pain and jealousy and rejection and how and why men and women hurt each other. The house was no longer his, but hadn't he bought it? And had he not returned to find another man in his place? One wonders how much loneliness and frustration and heartache and wounded pride went into each jealous swing of the axe.

In a moment the door was nearly demolished. He kicked open what was left of it and walked into the center of the room. He stood there with the axe in his hand, breathing heavily from the exertion, saying nothing. His estranged wife and her lover stood numbly in front of the couch where they'd been sitting. The TV was on. Tense seconds passed.

At length the intruding troubadour regained his composure. He looked at his wife's companion and said calmly, "I just wanted to know who you are and what you look like."

Then he turned and left.

From my own store of jealousy follies, let me give you an example of a rival's jealous rage. When the following episode occurred, I had just been involved with a woman who was living with and deceiving another man, and had found the arrangement most unsatisfactory for my emotional needs. I have since concluded that it is unwise for me to conduct secret affairs of this sort though I can understand how this situation may suit others.

One evening soon after I reached this conclusion, I met a young woman I'll call Maryanne at a friend's house. I was immediately attracted to her and she to me. She was bright, warm, and had a good sense of humor—at least she liked my jokes. A month earlier Maryanne had separated from her husband Frank, established a separate residence, and filed for final divorce papers. I thought, at last, here's a woman with no entanglements. We can start off relatively fresh. But her estranged husband had other ideas.

Although I'd met Maryanne long after their domestic problems caused her to leave him and file for divorce, her husband began to blame me for their problems, and saw me as a barrier to their reconciliation. Somehow he'd obtained my telephone number and called her several times when she was visiting me. On one of these occasions he asked to speak to me, began the conversation with a proprietary "This is Maryanne's husband," and demanded that I stop seeing her. I loved her, felt morally correct in seeing her, and felt no inclination or obligation whatsoever to comply with his request.

Maryanne's soon-to-be ex-husband regularly patrolled the street where she'd moved and became more and more incensed at seeing my car often parked in front of her house. I was well along into research for this book by then, knew what jealousy could do to otherwise rational people, and began to worry a bit. When he made disparaging remarks or even uttered threats against my life to her, I could pass them off as normal jealousy. But then he threatened to kill her and himself. This was during the week of the mass murder-suicides of the People's Temple cult in Guyana and the shooting deaths of San Francisco's Mayor George Moscone and Supervisor Harvey Milk. We were just across the bay and the atmosphere in our area was somewhat tense.

I was at Maryanne's house early one morning when the telephone rang. Her husband again. He needed to exchange cars. I remained upstairs in bed while she met him at the door with the keys, but he pushed her aside and stormed into the house. He'd seen my car and knew I was there. I looked around the room futilely for some kind of weapon. Next to the bed, in one of my pants pockets, was my tiny Swiss army knife. I took out the knife and opened the larger blade as the footsteps grew louder. Here I was, about to participate in the primordial jealousy scene.

The husband stomped into the room and stood over the bed. I lay there naked under the covers, feeling at a definite disadvantage. From my perspective near the floor he seemed very large, and I had no doubt that he was agitated. He was wearing boots, jeans, and a blue down-filled vest. His right hand gripped something in the right vest pocket.

"I thought I told you to stay away from Maryanne!" he began.

No good could come from arguing with him, so I said nothing. I was confronted by a jealous, agitated man unwilling and unable to accept a true loss. I was aware of feeling some fear, but mostly I was in a state of hyper-alertness. I knew I needed all my resources to deal with this situation. Had he attacked me physically I would have done my best to disable him or worse. But no verbal provocation could have moved me to violence.

Maryanne entered briefly, then left the room. Had she remained, the situation would have surely exploded immediately. I kept my eyes fixed on his.

"What is it you want, just someone to fuck? Or are you going to tell me you love her?" asked the husband. I did love her, but I saw no good in pursuing that question with him at the time. Again, I said nothing.

"Or do you just hate me?" he continued.

This surprised me. Although I'd been annoyed at what seemed an unreasonable interference in my affair, I certainly had no hatred for the man. So for the first time I spoke.

"I don't hate you, Frank." My voice was soft and seemed a bit shaky to me. His stance became less rigid. "If I had the guts I'd just throw you out that window," he replied, and walked out of the room. Just as I had zipped up my trousers, he returned and glowered at me. At that moment two sheriff's deputies arrived. While Frank and I were considering life and death, Maryanne had telephoned the authorities. The deputies warned Frank he'd be arrested if he entered the house again without permission.

Frank, Maryanne, and I all hold advanced graduate

degrees and practice professionally in our communities. We're not violence-prone, yet an ugly situation was only narrowly averted.

So don't chastise yourself too much when jealousy strikes. It happens in the best of families.

4 Sleuthing

A man hires a private detective to follow his wife and her lover. The detective reports: "They went to the show together, then to a nightclub, then to another nightclub, and came home in a taxi half-drunk. Then they went up to his apartment. I climbed up on the fire escape and watched them through the window. They drank some more and he chased her around the table and threw her on the hearth-rug in front of the fire and took off all her clothes with his teeth. Then he carried her into the bedroom with her pants hanging on one ankle. The shades were down in the bedroom, and so that's all I saw."

"That's it!" says the husband, striking himself on the forehead. "That's *it*! Always that doubt!" (from *Rationale of the Dirty Joke* by G. Legman, Grove Press, 1968)

Just as jealousy is often the shadow of love, so does shadowing frequently accompany jealousy. Scratch a jealous lover and you'll likely find a budding detective. You may be surprised or comforted to learn how common it is for jealous people to spy on their lovers. Jealousy often transforms ordinary citizens into amateur gumshoes, some cunning, some clumsy. Whatever their detective skills, they share a mighty urge to learn just what the loved one is doing, when, and with whom. An overwhelming compulsion rises up in them to find out whether their jealous suspicions are really true, to learn the identity of the rival, and to see what he or she is all about.

How does the sleuthing process begin? Usually it's preceded by suspicion, by discovering possible "evidence" a partner may be seeing someone else. It could be little things, like a strand of hair on a sweater, or puzzling message units on the phone bill, or perhaps a few casually explained late evenings at work.

Maybe nothing is really wrong, but once those jealous thoughts begin they're difficult to ignore. In fact, they may occupy one's mind day and night. Should the lover be confronted with these suspicions? Perhaps they're baseless. Bringing jealous accusations into a relationship may well cause what is most feared. "Where there's smoke, there's fire" usually means fire has preceded the smoke. In the case of jealousy, smoke may produce the fire. Jealousy implies the existence of a rival. Raising the issue can plant the idea in a loved one's mind. If a man is accused of being interested in another woman, as in "I saw you smiling meaningfully at her!" he may then think on some level, "Gee, maybe I was interested in her and didn't know it. Maybe she's interested in me, too."

So the jealous person might avoid a confrontation of this type and secretly begin looking for clues. Finally there's a surrender to the impulse to investigate.

Eleanor is a former high school chemistry teacher married twelve years to a lawyer. They have two children. Eleanor was in her early forties when she slipped into the sleuth slough. Her investigative techniques were rather sophisticated. "My husband regularly spends most of his Saturdays playing golf, but one Sunday when I was putting his golf shoes back in the closet I noticed there was no mud or grass on the cleats. Then I remembered he hadn't mentioned meeting any of his friends at the course. The next day when I was using the station wagon I noticed a filtered cigarette butt in the ashtray. I was deliberately searching now. There was no lipstick on them but they were Virginia Slims cigarettes. I remember thinking a little bitterly, You've come a long way, baby!

"From that point on, there was no stopping me. I drove round trip to the golf course to determine the mileage, then checked the odometer on the car after he'd used it on Saturdays. Twice during the following four Saturdays there were fifteen unexplained miles. Then, after he'd made a three-day business trip to New Orleans, I found in one of his trouser pockets a box of matches from a little romantic restaurant we always go to when we're down there together. I thought he would certainly have mentioned going there if he'd had nothing to hide. I even checked the small jar of Vaseline he keeps in his shaving kit. The Vaseline was unused before he left, and now it had a big gouge in it, plus a small curly strand of blonde hair.

"It was only a matter of time before I got up the nerve to follow him one Saturday. I borrowed a friend's nondescript VW bug and wore a hat and dark glasses, then waited at a nearby gas station for him to pass. My God, I was so scared he'd notice me and yet I was exhilarated. I followed him to a suburban apartment village about seven miles from town and watched as he pulled into a numbered parking stall behind a Mustang. He locked the car and walked into an inner courtyard. I parked down the street and waited about forty-five minutes to see whether he'd come out with someone. When he didn't I went home. The following Monday afternoon I drove back to the apartment village. I checked the name on the mailbox of the apartment connected with the parking stall. It turned out to be a single woman living there alone. I remember feeling all at once triumphant, sad, confused, and let down. It was so anticlimactic at that point I also felt ashamed.''

Eleanor waited a week, then calmly confronted her husband. The news that she'd been following him was met with shock and outrage. They had an argument lasting most of the night. "I don't think I'd ever want to go through another detective episode," she said. "Nothing changed except that we were able to rekindle our relationship for a while. Now it's rocky again.''

When one of my neighbors learned I was collecting stories about jealousy, she wrote to her mother about the project. She received a lengthy letter in reply, containing several tales of nonmilitary espionage during the World War II years. The mother's letter had a confessional character to it, as if she wanted to share these past adventures with her daughter.

Your father and I were living in Birmingham, Alabama, in 1942. He had stayed out late one night and I suspected him of stepping out with a woman who lived a block away. I went there in the dead of night and sneaked around the back of the house and peeked through the window. There they were, sure enough, locked in oral sex. I was furious. I couldn't get in through the doors, so I jumped for an open window of the bedroom, managing to get a leg over the sill and boost myself in. I immediately leaped into the middle of their lovemaking and started screaming, fighting, and scratching to beat all hell. Then I ran out the front door.

Another time he was mixed up with someone named Mary Jo who he claimed worked for his company and was "just some old lady." She turned out to be a young woman who worked at the Georgia Dairy Bar. I took the trolley to Fourteenth Street and hung out for an hour or so until she got off work. I followed her home to her upstairs apartment, then went up and knocked on the door. When she answered I told her who I was and stuck my foot in the door. She was shocked, but I stayed long enough to tell her, "I only came to tell you you can have him." That night I told your father, "I went to see Mary Jo today." He threw a big soup spoon at me.

Once I suspected your father was having a fling with the company switchboard operator. He was just driving her to and from work, he said. I decided to find out the full story on my own. One morning I put a large cardboard box in the back seat of the car, telling him I planned to pick up some drapes from my aunt that evening. He paid no attention and went off to work. That afternoon, about an hour before quitting time, I went downtown to his office, unlocked the car with my set of keys, got into the back seat, and hid myself under the box. Sure enough, here came Bob and Miss PBX, right on schedule. They got in the car together. They were obviously lovers. At one point Bob reached in the back seat for a monkey wrench and felt all around the box before getting his hands on it. I was sure he would find me but he didn't. Later on, when he returned home and entered the house, I waited a few minutes, then got out of the car and walked into the house beaming. I had the goods on him and I was really happy.

My neighbor told me she was delighted her mother finally had shared such stories with her after so many years. "You know," she added, "Mom made a lot of noise about Dad's affairs, but after she'd done something dramatic to show him she knew about them, she never left him. She loved him too much, I guess."

One night, over too many Irish coffees at an outdoor café, a popular disc jockey admitted using his knowledge of electronics to spy on a girl friend:

"My life was at loose ends at the time. I was seeing a young woman who had the habit of occasionally disappearing for two or three days. I would become incredibly jealous and tense, so much that I started reading her diary. I checked the dates she had disappeared and also those when she had taken a short trip to Denver and Salt Lake City. She would write that she went to a film with John or Harry and after the entry she wrote 'NYE.' I didn't know what that meant until I remembered her telling me of the first sexual experience she'd had, about a year before meeting me. It'd been on New Year's Eve with a guy who had held her down on a bathroom floor for about three hours. 'NYE' (New Year's Eve) was her code for making love. Once when she'd disappeared for a day, I knew she had met three guys at an art fair in the city. She'd gone back to an apartment with them for the day and had gotten it on with them all in some kind of semi-orgy. The diary said 'Richard and Ron and Ron—NYE.' I found this out after she'd discovered she was pregnant. I didn't know if the child was mine and I was flipping out.

"I tapped her phone. I had access to some bugging equipment and installed it at the master telephone lug box in the basement of her apartment building. I just unscrewed her telephone line, plugged in the bug, which was a little box the size of a pack of cigarettes, then connected the bug to the lug box. It would pick up her telephone conversations and broadcast them for about two hundred feet to a special FM receiver—beautiful reception.

"I didn't stop there. I had a microphone taped on the wall of her bedroom closet—a very sensitive one that would pick up conversations anywhere within thirty feet and broadcast them up to a mile. One day when I was there I checked the mike and found it had fallen down. She had no idea what it was. She thought it was something from the lights. She didn't know. People just don't imagine they're going to be bugged.

"I never did record the conversations. I just listened. After a while it became pathological. My whole life was centered around being next to my listening equipment day and night. It became an end in itself. I wanted to hear everything. Just to find out. Actually I learned far more from her diary than anything else but I couldn't stop. The desire to hear everything that's going on just overcomes you.

"Finally after five weeks or so I stopped the bugging. A while later after she'd had an abortion, I told her I knew she had fucked all three of those guys. She said, 'So what, what're you going to do about it?' She thought I was a little insane, and she was probably right. My desire to know everything could have been masochistic, I don't know. It must have been, although even now I don't feel I intentionally wanted to be hurt. But there seems no other logical explanation for wanting to know every detail. We stayed together somehow for two more months. It's hard to imagine how intense it all was."

A surprising number of jealous individuals believe sleuthing is best done by professionals. I am indebted to the Belli and Choulos law firm for this information. Vasilios Choulos introduced me to a tough-talking young private detective who informed me jealousy accounts for a significant portion of his work. So it was that I found myself a few weeks later outside the picturesque office of Craig Zurkey, private eye.

The scene was reminiscent of vintage Warner Bros. detective movies—an enclosed pier adjacent to railroad tracks on a little-traveled section of the San Francisco waterfront. Foghorns boomed through the cold, wet air. I stood for a moment outside the arched pier entrance shivering in the gloom, then ventured inside. Zurkey welcomed me to his office and invited me to sit down. I switched on my tape recorder. He did the same with his.

The going rate for private detectives at the time was $25 an hour, or $250 for a twenty-four-hour surveillance. Zurkey says he always gets cash "up front" in jealousy cases.

"In this type of work and in criminal work, you always stay ahead of it, moneywise. Because almost always, whatever happens—if you succeed in your job or you don't—they're just not going to be happy and you're liable to get screwed later on."

The majority of Zurkey's jealousy cases are women hiring him to follow a man. He thinks jealous women hire him more often because men may feel more capable of doing their own surveillance. Most of these women are single and don't have a live-in relationship with their men. They tend to be between thirty and fifty years old and seem to differ from other women only in that they have enough money to contract for investigative services.

"I guess jealousy more than anything else just makes you crazy. You can't think rationally. Typically a woman even confronts the guy and says, 'Hey, are you fooling around?' And he'll say no. But on the other hand she *knows* he is. Well, what's her next move? Every so often, if they have the money, they'll come to private investigators. They just *want* to *know*."

Most of Zurkey's clients are referred by lawyers and

others who routinely employ him. The process usually begins with a telephone call from an excited, nervous woman inquiring about "a tail job." Procedures and fees are explained and arrangements made for a meeting with the new client. Prior to getting together with the investigator, the client is asked to write down as much as possible about the person to be observed—habits, friends, place of work, where he eats and sleeps, and especially his car and license-plate number. A photograph of the subject is very useful too. Sometimes the client can afford to hire an investigator for three or four days or longer. But if money is a problem, Zurkey can almost always get the information desired within twenty-four hours.

"We can very easily trick him into making his move on any given night. What I usually suggest is that she spend a whole week with this guy, day and night, until he's so bored with her he can't stand it. And then all of a sudden give him three days' notice that she has to go out of town for a day, so he thinks she's going to be far gone. In fact, I tell her to actually get out of town if it's convenient. That's when he's going to make his move. I remember one case where I never did catch the guy fooling around. But that's only one. If they're serious enough to put up the money, the guy is almost always fooling around. That's what I've found. And you know, it's quite easy to catch them."

Zurkey defines the art of surveillance as seeing just how close one can get to a subject without being "burned" (recognized).

"You know, I've been in bars and restaurants, right in the next booth, back to back with the guy and a microphone held up like this. It's great if you can hear a conversation. If you can hear it, you can also tape it. Tapes and photographs are very big in these cases."

Electronic bugging devices in private investigations are

now illegal, so if the client wishes detailed information about how the rival lives, Zurkey says he uses simple techniques. His car might "break down" outside the rival's house and he'll ask to use the telephone.

"You just get inside, look around, maybe strike up a little bit of a conversation, and that's all you need.

"Just about the most interesting case I've had like this was a thirty-five-year-old woman, involved with a thirty-year-old guy. He was real good-looking, a stud. And she was quite sure he was fooling around. She had found little notes in his wallet and his pockets. You know, 'Kathy' and a phone number, or part of a phone number, something like that. There was one thing really strange about it. It almost seemed like he was leaving clues that there were other women in his life. But when I checked these clues out they were always dead ends. These women did not exist. The addresses did not exist. The phone numbers did not exist. It was very strange. So we set the guy up and she went out of town. So here we go. One night I'm outside his place and he's got this brand-new white Corvette—I'll never forget it. I had a seventy-one Toyota. So he gets in his car, I get in mine, and he takes off. I think we ended up in Petaluma, fifty miles away. And man, this guy was going like ninety, one hundred miles an hour. And my car was just shimmying all the way and I almost said the hell with it because my car just couldn't go any faster and I thought it was going to fall apart.

"Well, I successfully followed him and here he goes to this little country home. And I was able to get a really good vantage point on him. I'm a couple hundred yards away. I see him pull in the driveway. I stop my car and get out the binoculars and I'm watching him. He knocks on the door. The door opens. And a man comes to the door.

"He stayed all night. The blinds were drawn, so I just watched all night. When he left the next morning, I just went and had some breakfast and waited a few more hours. And then I did the old car-broke-down routine. I got into the house and there was only a guy there, as far as I could tell. This guy started making passes at me. He's giving me the eye and all that. That was the scene. The guy was obviously gay. So I reported this to my client and a very strange thing happend at that point—she got mad at *me* for some reason. She was obviously very, very humiliated. And I said, 'Well, these are the facts, this is what happened.' She was sure I was wrong. She said, 'Well, obviously you must have fallen asleep and there was a woman there. Did you go through the whole house?' And I said, 'No,' and she said, 'There had to be a woman there because I'm sure he's not gay.' Well, one thing led to another and she hired me once more—I think it was a sequence of three two-hour surveillances after he got off work. The guy was hanging out at a gay bar. I followed him in once and he had all kinds of friends, you know, patting on the ass, kissing, the whole schmeer. So that was that case.''

According to Zurkey, jealous people who hire private investigators are usually sure their lovers have other interests. Besides confirming this fact, they want to know what the competition is like. He's asked to report on the rival's living situation, physical appearance, and especially financial status. Since his clients usually are fairly well off financially, money is a level they can easily compete on. Since they often feel their lovers are stepping out on them because of some shortcoming, photographs and tape recordings of the rival are valued information. The client wants to know if her rival has something that she lacks. Perhaps she'll try using this information to give the missing ingredient to the man.

But Zurkey thinks usually it's just a question of ''variety being the spice of life. It's a very dominant force in society and that's usually where it's at. Most of the time I walk away from a job thinking, geez, it'd almost be better if she didn't know. Because once everything is confirmed there's probably going to be fireworks within their relationship. She's going to have this volcano inside her and confront him and say, 'Look, man, I had a private investigator follow you. And I *know*. Here are the photographs. Here's the tape recording.' So what happens? The guy's going to be totally humiliated and chances are they're going to break up. Whereas in the first place he didn't love his lady any less. He's just trying to get a little on the side.''

Obviously Zurkey is capable of spying on his own girl friends and he admitted doing so in the past. He didn't admit to spying on his current girl friend, a beautiful young woman I found very attractive. Very attractive, Zurkey.

The last time I saw *him* was at a—what else?—*surprise* birthday party for a mutual friend. Zurkey was posted at the front window peering through the side of a window shade, waiting for the guest of honor.

Craig Zurkey learned his craft from Hal Lipset, dean of American private investigators. Among his many feats, Lipset invented the famed olive-in-the-martini bugging device, was chief investigator for Sam Dash on the Senate Watergate committee, and served as technical consultant for Francis Coppola's award-winning film *The Conversation*. Hal Lipset is a gravelly-voiced man who looks like (and is, I think) somebody's Jewish grandfather. He lives and works in a stylish Victorian mansion containing a futuristic electronics laboratory.

Before no-fault divorce laws, surveillance cases usually were attempts to get an edge on a spouse in court battles.

Now, says Lipset, "anyone who has their spouse or lover followed does it because of jealousy."

Why?

"Ego. No woman or man can accept the fact they have been supplanted in the affections of the other half of the relationship—any relationship—without having a very difficult ego problem. Ego desires an answer to 'Who took my place?' and 'Why?' Rarely is it 'Where did I fail?' I've had some clients for as long as ten years who constantly want to know who's the new person in the spouse's life. They don't recognize it as jealousy but there is no other real motive.

"In many cases, not only do they want to find out who the other party is, but they want to *see* the person. I've had people ask me to take them out—and from a distance where they couldn't be seen—because they wanted to see the other woman and their husband, or the other man their wife was with. Then they want to sit down and talk at great length about why this happened. And they want to go through all the details of their relationship. You become a psychiatrist.

"Sometimes they don't believe you. Sometimes you get real paranoiacs, who think somebody's following them, that they're being investigated when they're really not being investigated. Sometimes they think you've sold out to the other side and you're covering up for them. You never satisfy anybody in a situation like this.

"But jealousy suspicions are usually founded. As an investigator, a private detective, I find it hard to believe there's such a thing as monogamy."

Monogamous couples may be an endangered species, but shadowing a spouse can somtimes turn up entirely unexpected evidence. Among the cases Hall Lipset discussed was that of a woman suspicious of her husband's early-day whereabouts. Each morning there was an unexplained gap of time before he arrived at work. Believing he was having an affair, the woman engaged Lipset to do surveillance. After following the man every morning for ten days, Lipset concluded that all he wanted was a quiet place to have breakfast and read the newspaper for an hour before going to work.

No-fault divorces represent a major change in our concept of marriage as an everlasting institution. I asked attorney Vasilios Choulos if this change had perhaps altered his clients' responses to infidelity. "No, no. The mechanics of jealousy are still there. In my practice I discourage people from hiring investigators in divorce cases because the dollars simply aren't there. Why waste the money? *But the people themselves still want to know.* They want the opportunity to be able to prove, get mad, and go through the process of feeling sorry for themselves, of being taken advantage of, then projecting all this on the other party. No, it's still there. I'm afraid you're not going to be able to legislate jealousy away."

This urge to know leads some people into situations at once absurd, hilarious, and humiliating. A Columbia, Missouri, obstetrical nurse told me the following story about three of her friends.

Mitchell and Jane were a young married couple of modest means who rented out a room in their house to Ed, a young writer. Ed lived frugally and had few possessions except for his clothes, which frequently needed mending. Mitchell began to suspect Ed and Jane were carrying on an affair. Jane denied it. She said she just felt sorry for Ed and sometimes helped take care of his tattered clothing.

But Mitch became more and more suspicious. One afternoon he arranged to leave work early and came home unannounced at 2:00 P.M. As he approached the house, he looked up at his second-floor bedroom window and saw his tenant framed in the window, obviously sitting on the edge of Mitch and Jane's bed. Only the naked upper half of Ed's body was visible, but Mitch could see his right arm moving back and forth in a gentle stroking motion.

Mitch opened the front door, raced up the stairs cursing, and crashed through his bedroom door. Ed was alone. A shirt began to scorch on the ironing board he'd been using. Jane customarily placed the board across the bed when she ironed her clothes. She had insisted Ed use it while she went shopping for the day. Years passed before Mitch could speak about his mistake to anyone.

Sleuthing is a specialized form of the jealousy follies, a common but avoidable waste of time and human spirit. To a mind consumed by jealousy and suspicion, following a loved one may seem better than doing nothing, but it never has a happy outcome. Either the suspicions will be confirmed or the sleuth will only think more detective work is needed.

One college woman I interviewed suspected, when her professor husband's affection waned, that he was having an affair. She looked through his briefcase and found a copy of a letter to one of his ex-lovers describing the ecstasies of an extramarital affair he was presently conducting. This discovery added nothing to the relationship between the college professor and his wife, but did add fuel to the fiery arguments that ultimately consumed their relationship.

Even when sleuthing is recognized as an absurd activity degrading to all concerned, it may be as hard to resist as it is to ignore jealous thoughts once they begin. I had a taste of it myself and know the feeling.

During the 1960s I was living in Berkeley, at the beginning of the current period of cultural and emotional ferment and experimentation. I lived on what had been the grounds of Williams College, a small defunct avant-garde liberal-arts college not connected with the Eastern school of the same name. My home, Farley Hall, had once been the music building. The girl friend of a friend occupying the Science Building had several times spent the night with me at Farley Hall with his knowledge and approval. At the time I wondered how I would feel were I in his place. Soon I had an opportunity to find out.

I had met an attractive San Francisco journalist and fashion designer. We both dated others but sometimes she would spend the night with me in Berkeley. Inevitably she met my male Science Building friend, then living alone. One day I arranged to meet her at my house—she would do her work there until I arrived. Returning earlier than expected, I found she wasn't there. Was she working on Science instead, I wondered? I walked uphill to the Science Building, approached the front door stealthily, and peered through a crack in the worn slats. Sure enough, she was sitting on the edge of my friend's bed. They were both nude. I left the Science Building as quickly and quietly as I could, baffled by my feelings. Hadn't my friend willingly shared his girl friend with me? Didn't I see other women as well as my journalist friend? Yet I was undeniably jealous. I felt betrayed, hurt. Later she told me they'd only taken their clothes off, nothing more. Maybe. Either way my feelings were unreasonable. That's when I first learned jealousy seldom yields to logic.

There's a way to avoid the jealousy follies. It begins with understanding what jealousy is all about, and why it affects some people more than others. With this knowledge as a basis, you and those you love can learn how to put painful, irrational, jealous thoughts and behavior out of your lives.

Don't expect this change to happen immediately, even when you've read all I have to say on the subject. You've got some hard work to do first. But you can quickly relieve the pain of jealousy right now. In medicine we speak of palliation and cure. Easing the pain of a broken arm with medication is palliation. Setting and casting the arm is the cure. I've put together a Jealousy FIrst-Aid Kit, easily carried and implemented. Use it for emergencies while you're working on the cure.

5   The Jealousy
First-Aid Kit

Once gripped by jealousy, most people can't think clearly about their dilemma. Preoccupied by their pain, they run events and individuals over and over again through their minds. Later, you'll learn methods for limiting unwarranted jealousy to an occasional nuisance. But if you've suffered a surprise attack of jealousy, you need a way out now, even if it's only temporary relief.

1. ADMIT TO YOUR JEALOUSY

That's right, admit to yourself that you are jealous. You may very likely be ashamed and guilty for having the emotion at all (one of the great double binds of our time). Don't feel guilty. Do be kind to yourself. Those who turn their backs on jealousy, denying its existence, rarely prevent the axe from falling. They merely succeed in not watching. Relieving the pain of jealousy begins with acknowledging that it's a valid emotion, that it's a normal part of growing, and that it can be a key to greater self-understanding. Certainly there's no reason to feel shame or guilt.

Because jealousy so often accompanies feelings of insecurity, chances are you'll be tempted to slide into bitter self-criticism. You may find yourself dwelling on the flood of shortcomings (real or fancied) that you believe have made you less attractive and less worthy of love. This kind of grim introspection is absolutely the last thing you need now. Simply admit to yourself that what you're feeling is jealousy.

2. ESCAPE

Don't let anyone convince you otherwise, the best escape is escape. Take a short vacation—across the street, across town, or across the country, depending on your circumstances and inclination. True, you can't always run away from pain, but you *can* physically remove yourself from the place where you have experienced traumatic events. A few days in the country or by the water can do a lot of good. A friend described his getaway:

> Nancy told me she wanted to be on her own for a while and I really had no choice but to agree. She'd met someone else but neither of us talked about it. I didn't want to blow the chances for our getting back together by flying into a jealous rage, but I made sure she understood how much I loved her. I remember coming back to my apartment feeling very tense, almost to the point of being physically sick. Nancy seemed to be everywhere. There were the candles she'd given me and the records we listened to while making love. There was the bedspread, the pillows, everthing. Every time I turned around, there was some little thing reminding me of her—and that just

kicked the agony up another notch. I had to get out of there in a hurry.

So I called Jerry, an old friend who had a small ranch in Mendocino, California, and he told me to come right down. And that's what I did—threw a few things in my car and drove all night to get there. Jerry kept me busy the next ten days chopping wood and helping him build a chicken coop. When I went back to Portland I was able to talk to Nancy without feeling poisoned by jealous feelings.

Some months later the couple resumed their relationship on a much stronger footing.

3. SLEEP

Get a good night's sleep. No doubt about it, a solid night's sleep helps to restore physical and psychological equilibrium, leaving you better prepared to tackle the next round. If you can't get to sleep, this is one occasion when a sedative or a couple of drinks may be of timely assistance. However, these should be considered as only temporary measures.

A hot bath or a sauna is an excellent way to reduce muscular tension and achieve relaxation prior to sleeping. If you have a friend to give you a back massage, you are fortunate indeed. Otherwise, try to find a health spa where you can get a sauna bath and a no-nonsense massage.

4. TALK OUT YOUR FEELINGS

Getting it off your chest can be very constructive. Talk to someone who is sympathetic but uninvolved in your situation. The best candidate is someone who will listen carefully and share viewpoints. If that person happens to have more experience with jealousy than you, so much the better. It's possible the person who turns out to be most helpful may not know you well but instead has a good understanding of human behavior and can share insights.

Choose wisely. Avoid anyone who might secretly enjoy your discomfort or who may have some interest in the personalities involved. In short, choose someone you trust. Avoid talking about your plight to casual friends and acquaintances. Otherwise you might hear such wonderful advice as "Don't be jealous" or "You're only jealous because you're insecure, so stop being so insecure"—always nice to hear when you're on the ropes bleeding.

One immediate advantage to confiding your thoughts is that you may discover you've been misinterpreting your partner's behavior, that in fact your suspicion is groundless. Talk out your feelings thoroughly, and once you've done so, *stop talking about it*.

5. WRITE OUT YOUR FEELINGS

Put your emotions on paper. Describe your feelings carefully and fully—rejection, anger, fear of loss, fear of being left alone, desire for revenge, competitiveness, resentment, and so forth. The objective here is to develop a clearer understanding of exactly how you feel. Call it organizing your jealousy.

You may find this easiest to do in the form of a letter— one of those letters you don't mail. You'll be amazed at how much you can learn about yourself and your feelings and how much relief is possible simply by laying your thoughts out on paper.

6. MEDITATE ON YOUR JEALOUSY—
BY APPOINTMENT ONLY

Rather than allowing the monster to consume you, cozy up to it. Paradoxically, by confronting it eye to eye you can put distance between you and all those painful emotions. Here's how to do it.

Get comfortable in a place where you won't be distracted for a few minutes. Consciously relax your body, starting at your toes and moving toward your troubled head, muscle by muscle, limb by limb. Put aside all cares and concerns except for IT (your jealous feelings). This should be quite easy, since IT has been hogging most of your attention anyway, right? Now for a few moments deliberately think about the character and intensity of all those painful feelings until you can sense a distinction between you and those feelings. "Here I am" and "There are the emotions I'm feeling." Ask yourself, "Is this agony unendurable? Is it really *that* bad?" It's bad, all right, but you will find that this contemplative separation of feelings allows you to understand with greater clarity that it's not the end of the world, that you can and will survive. More importantly, you'll begin to realize you can maintain your true self even within an emotional hurricane.

The above exercise is based on yoga concentration techniques for achieving mastery over the restless, easily distracted mind. In fact, if you're used to the daily practice of meditation, it can be a very useful aid in minimizing pain and cultivating strength and insight. The advantage of this exercise is that instead of allowing jealousy to hound you in the guise of a vaguely defined menace, you are deliberately setting aside time to turn and squarely face the beast, to confront it, and thus diminish its power to hurt you. You may be reluctant to deliberately court such a confrontation, but with just a little practice it can be a surprisingly effective method.

Each time you complete this exercise, say to yourself, "Okay, I've given it my full attention, I've looked at it, and I'm putting it out of my mind for a while." If jealousy invades your thoughts when you're not doing this exercise, remember you've made an appointment with yourself to think about it another time. This way you begin to effectively control your jealousy. You are not running from your feelings but instead develop the power to deal with them on *your* terms at your convenience. Do this exercise once or twice a day for a few minutes only. Then put jealousy out of your mind until your next appointment with it.

7. DON'T THINK TOO MUCH—KEEP BUSY

As we've seen in the chapter on sleuthing, an imagination fired by jealousy knows no bounds. The jealous mind can conjure up every conceivable variation on the theme "Oh God, what are they doing now?" If you allow it, you can occupy all your time embroidering endless answers to countless questions. You can get incredibly worked up improvising the most elaborate scenarios. It's like starring in your own horror movie, and no matter what the ending, you lose. This can be a particularly cruel torture. Recognize temptation and make a habit of walking out on your own B-movies.

Keep busy! This is a cardinal rule of jealousy first aid and it would be hard to overemphasize its value. Don't lie brooding in bed in the morning. Make sure your schedule is full of events and tasks that are satisfying and fully occupy your thoughts. Here are some suggestions:

1. Work out physically. Recent research confirms commonsense knowledge that exercise produces a feeling of well-being. Besides, almost any strenuous physical activity will relieve tension. Don't overdo it; don't push yourself beyond your present physical limits.

But remember that regular exercise will make you look and feel better. Choose the exercise best suited for you. It might be jogging, swimming, or lifting weights. Dancing is an excellent way to exercise in a social setting. Competitive games like tennis will absorb your attention completely.

2. Get involved in a game you enjoy—chess, billiards, bridge, poker, backgammon. Avoid backbiting.

3. Paint a room.

4. Rearrange your furniture.

5. See a good film; attend a lecture at the local college.

6. Cook elaborate meals and give small dinner parties.

As a by-product of some of these activities, you'll become more interesting and meet new people.

Remember, you've got better things to do with your valuable time than ruminate on jealousy. Keep busy!

8. READ WISE COUNSEL

Many of us are familiar with spiritual or philosophical works that can provide solace and a sense of perspective. When jealousy causes deep suffering, take time to read such literature, and you'll find the stories, poetry, or commentary can help pull you away from your discomforting thoughts. The many fine books by Alan Watts are a great celebration of existence, full of compassion and grace. A good choice for the stress of jealousy would be his book *The Book: On the Taboo Against Knowing Who You Are*.

Watt's principal philosophic concern was to bring to the West the rich tradition and wisdom of Eastern religious thought. Others may read the religious philosopher Thomas Merton, whose *No Man Is an Island* is a compassionate understanding of the predicament and destiny of the human spirit. There are many such writings, but one I particularly recommend is *The Light Within*, a collection of the thoughts of Dr. Albert Schweitzer culled from his seven major books.

Many Westerners find comforting insights in two classic Chinese books now widely available in the West: The *Tao Te Ching* by Lao Tzu, a renowned teacher and contemporary of Confucius, is a collection of poetic and deeply spiritual commentaries; the *I Ching* is both a rich distillation of centuries of Chinese thought and a much-revered oracle. Regardless of the counsel you turn to, bear in mind that your suffering, however intense at the moment, is sure to pass soon, that it is ultimately a brief episode on life's larger stage.

One young woman, a broadcast journalist by profession, claimed to have found reassurance in the life-affirming passages of "Desiderata," until it was transformed into a popular inspirational wall poster and a hit record. "I used to gain solace from the passage 'You are a child of the universe, you have a right to be here,' " she said. "But after the *National Lampoon* spoofed the record with their own version, I kept hearing, 'You are a fluke of the universe, you have no right to be here.' So much pain and there I was laughing." Which brings us to the next to last and most elusive item in the jealousy first-aid kit: laughter.

9. LAUGH

Laughter is a good way to deal with jealousy. To laugh at oneself is to mock the beast, if not to slay it. One momentarily confronts all those brutal images and strips them of their power.

"It's an old story, I guess. She done left me for another man. I was really down. Everyone tried to cheer me up in the usual ways. Everyone except Larry Hankin, the actor and comedian, he had a difference approach." A friend was recounting his struggles to deal with jealousy and rejection. "One evening Larry came by and we went out for a drink. He listened patiently to my woes until I happened to mention in passing that this was the first time I'd been badly burned. He looked surprised.

" 'Wait a minute,' he interrupted. 'How old are you?'

" 'Thirty-two,' I answered.

" 'And this is the first time you've been on the short end? Hey man, screw you! Go ahead and suffer! I've been on the short end half my life!' I had to laugh but Larry didn't stop there: 'I'll betcha five bucks that right now, at this very minute, your girl friend and her new love are getting it on. I mean at this very second her long blonde hair is brushing against his stomach and her lips are lovingly caressing his member. Her eyes are closed in pleasure and he's arching his back as he screams in ecstasy. Just picture it! Right now they're doing it!'

"God, the images were *awful*! But I couldn't help laughing, really laughing. And at the time I felt a sense of relief. All those painful fantasies I was secretly harboring seemed somehow very absurd."

You can't plan it, it just happens. But when you can laugh at yourself, at your folly, the pain, the confusion, the despair, and the insanity of it all, you're well on your way back to rejoin the celebration.

If you can't laugh at yourself, laugh at something or someone else. Go to a funny movie or see a nightclub comic. Humor is ultimately based on tragedy and this may seem even more evident when you're blue. But once you're able to break through the gloom, laughter is therapeutic.

10. KEEP THIS LIST WITH YOU

Make sure you have an abbreviated version of the Jealousy First-Aid Kit with you at all times. Keep it in your purse or wallet and don't forget you've got it when you need it. Remember:

The Jealousy First-Aid Kit

1. Admit to your jealousy
2. Escape
3. Sleep
4. Talk out your feelings
5. Write out your feelings
6. Meditate on your jealousy—by appointment only
7. Don't think too much—keep busy
8. Read wise counsel
9. Laugh
10. Keep this list with you

The first-aid procedures given above are techniques designed to help you regain emotional equilibrium. It's quite possible you can put all of them into practice within a day or two; once you do, you'll be amazed at how much better you can feel. Now that you know how to deal with an emergency, you're ready to take definitive steps to eliminate jealousy forever as a destructive factor in your life.

6 Shrinking the Green-Eyed Monster

All the available evidence tells us that basic human feelings like jealousy have remained unchanged throughout time. More than three hundred years ago, the Sieur de la Chambre, physician to the lord chancellor of France, wrote that "Jealousie is a confusion of Love, of Hate, of Fear, and of Despair." Though centuries have passed we don't have a better definition today.

More than three hundred years after the Sieur de la Chambre wrote about jealousy, another physician defined it similarly, if less succinctly. Writing in the *Psychoanalytical Quarterly* in 1972, Dr. Philip M. Spielman described the emotion this way: "In jealousy one experiences apprehension, anxiety, suspicion, or mistrust concerning the loss of a highly valued possession or the diversion to another, a third person, of affection and love."

Writers and troubadours were the first psychologists. Great masterpieces of literature endure largely because they so accurately portray timeless human emotions.

Shakespeare and Tolstoy, for example, often incorporated shrewd observations of human behavior into their writings.

You may know the story of an army general stationed on the island of Cyprus who fell prey to jealousy. He disappointed one of his trusted lieutenants by choosing another soldier as chief of staff. The lieutenant took his revenge by convincing the general that the other soldier was having an affair with the general's wife. The lieutenant succeeded so well that in a jealous rage the general smothered his wife with a pillow while she lay sleeping. When the general discovered the lieutenant's treachery he stabbed him to death, then committed suicide in remorse.

Shakespeare's *Othello* remains a definitive statement on the nature of the "green-eyed monster which doth mock the meat it feeds on."

Tolstoy's "Kreutzer Sonata," set in nineteenth-century Russia, is another tale of jealousy that does not seem dated today. The "Kreutzer Sonata" tells of a man whose suspicion of his wife and a musician becomes a lethal obsession. In one scene, the musician has been invited to dine with the couple. On the surface all is calm, but from the husband's point of view a titanic struggle is taking place:

> There was a certain tension between us; I noted every word, every expression either of us used, and attributed special significance to it.
>
> I could not help confessing to myself that it was agony for me to be in his presence. "It all depends on me," I thought, "whether I shall ever see him again or not." But not to see him would mean that I was afraid of him. No, I was not afraid of him. That, I thought, would be too humiliating.
>
> I no longer allowed myself to be jealous. In the first place, I had already suffered so much from jealousy

that I was exhausted and needed a rest; in the second, I wanted to believe my wife's asseverations, and so I did. Despite the fact that I was not jealous, all during dinner and the part of the evening preceding the music, I could not relax and be myself with either of them, but kept watching their movements and glances.

Even then they had avoided each other's eyes; it was not until supper, when he poured her out a glass of soda water, that they glanced at each other and smiled ever so slightly. I remembered with horror having caught that glance and that fleeting smile.

The mad beast of jealousy roared in its den and tried to rush out, but I forced it back, so afraid was I of its brute force.

"What a low feeling jealousy is!" I said to myself.

Ultimately, the husband stabs his wife to death. But Tolstoy, the master storyteller and psychologist, never provides his readers with any real evidence of duplicity between the wife and the musician.

Jealousy is truly a "base" emotion. I believe this complex of emotions and reactions is derived from a protective instinct and that its expression is learned behavior influenced by environment.

In his *Descent of Man*, Charles Darwin wrote: "Most of the more complex emotions are common to the higher animals and ourselves. Everyone has seen how jealous a dog is of his master's affection, if lavished on any other creature; and I have observed the same fact with monkeys."

Psychologist William James stated flatly that jealousy is instinctive, a trait inherited from our animal ancestors.

In the *Sorcerers of Dobu*, R. F. Fortune (Margaret Mead's husband at one time) described a western Pacific island society in which jealousy was the foremost characteristic of the culture. The Dobus were poor, sorcery-ridden, and lived in small family groups largely hostile to one another. Their traditional courtship and marriage customs intensified mistrust and the fear of infidelity. Because of brief "matinee" sexual encounters in the bush, Fortune wrote,

> a husband in Dobu tends to fall into the habit of mentally timing his wife when she goes off in the performance of the natural functions. Extreme jealousy takes the form of the husband who insists on going with his wife into the bush when she goes to exercise the natural functions.

Other anthropologists thought Alaskan Eskimos, Australian aborigines, and other groups were free of jealousy because they sometimes engaged in wife-lending on the visit of an honored guest. The anthropologists were right in this instance, but were wrong in thinking that these groups did not experience jealousy under other circumstances. Jealousy is an innate and universal human characteristic, but its specific cause may vary from one culture to another.

The potential of sexual acts to trigger jealous feelings depends on the *meaning* attached to those acts. Within our own culture, sexual swingers provide an example of sexual sharing not causing jealousy, provided the mates adhere to certain codes of behavior—like not becoming emotionally involved with their other sexual partners.

Dr. George DeVos, professor of anthropology at the University of California at Berkeley and an authority on both Japan and the Arab world, said during an interview for this book that Japanese men are generally not very jealous of their wives.

"You seldom even hear of instances of delusional or paranoid jealousy. The culture pattern is for women to be rather dedicated to acting within their roles. And in fact, this pattern is borne out statistically. They did the equivalent of a Kinsey study in Japan that revealed the rate of infidelity among Japanese women was around four percent. Japanese traditions are changing rapidly, but the concept of woman is one in which you can rely on her. She is self-regulating.''

And how do Japanese women feel about the long-standing tradition of their husbands having mistresses? There are those who are jealous and those who are quite philosophical about the practice—or rather expect it, said Dr. DeVos.

"Traditionally Japanese women accept their husband's behavior. This is less true overtly today but still true covertly. For instance, in some of their new religions, there are group-therapy sessions in which the theme will be how to handle a husband's infidelity. And the answer discussed will be something like, 'Men are very childlike and, just like infants, need their toys. Whereas the woman's self-perception is that she is more mature and can endure such foibles of childlike men.'

"Women, of course, are resentful of the man's phil-andering, but they don't use revenge, such as philandering against the husband. That's not a Japanese pattern. It has a lot to do with the very strong concept of belonging to the family in Japan. If there's a breakup, the man does not leave home. In other words, he can't lose a wife even if he wants to, because in doing so he loses a family. Nor can the wife lose the husband either, if she's faithful.''

Cultural norms of a society when measured against the standards of another society may seem pathological. While Japanese tradition regards women as mature and responsible, precisely the opposite view prevails in much of the Arab world. The Muslim practice of veiling women in public is largely based on vigilance against sexual infidelity. Muslim woman have traditionally been regarded as sexually vulnerable, childlike creatures having no internal resistance.

Consequently, they cannot be trusted and must be chaperoned in public at all times.

In studies of the Algerian personality conducted prior to the Algerian war, anthropologist Horace Minor noted a propensity for paranoia and pathological jealousy. Dr. DeVos, who helped analyze the data, says these tests reflected the Algerian attitudes of sexual vigilance so extreme—by our standards, anyway—that while some Algerians believed it was all right to have one's wife chaperoned by her mother, others didn't think the practice very safe. Given such exceptionally tight surveillance of wives, the rate of extramarital sex for women in Algeria is very likely even lower than that of wives in Japan, but unlike Japan, the potential for jealousy in Algeria is very high. "The simplest way to illustrate this," Dr. DeVos said, "is: if you ask a Japanese [man], 'What would you do if you found a strange man in your house?' he will reply, 'I'd ask him what he was doing there.' Ask the question of an Algerian and he'll reply: 'I'd kill him.' "

Other Muslim countries have less rigid sexual standards. This is true of Egypt, for example, particularly among the better educated classes. Oil money has recently had a part in lubricating Arab standards and provides an interesting link to Japan and the Middle East. Japanese cosmetic surgeons do a brisk business in revirgination. Among their international clientele are Arab women who fly to Japan to have their hymens restored before marriage.

While there is considerable variation from culture to culture in the kinds of behavior that provoke jealousy, one characteristic is found in common—a sense of property and ownership in relationships. We speak of "my husband," "my wife," or "my lover." Couples talk of belonging to each other. Sexual swinging sometimes reinforces the idea of love as property in that a person "gives" the love object to another. Where the love property secretly but indiscreetly gives sexual favors, however, jealousy is highly possible.

Loss, threatened loss, or imagined loss of a lover produces an intense reaction not only because our "property" is in danger but also because of a sense that this property contains part of ourself that is being torn away. René Descartes noted the relationship of jealousy and possession long ago when he wrote that jealousy was "a kind of fear related to a desire to preserve a possession."

Jealousy was, and is, a signal warning of a loss. Has this signal of loss lost its purpose? Perhaps. In this time of social experimentation, jealousy certainly can get in the way. But human life-spans and social experiments are brief compared with the survival of instincts. Thousands of years from now jealousy may possibly be as extinct as gasoline-powered engines, but the demise of the internal combustion motor is more certain than the snuffing of fires that feed jealousy. For jealousy has its roots in survival.

Some jealousy is normal and probably even useful. It is inordinate, unreasonable jealousy that should disturb us— jealousy that we know is unwarranted, that disturbs normal functioning. This kind of jealousy can be brought under control, but it's not easy when it has us by the psychic throat. That's the nature of this beast. If it were easily controlled, it wouldn't be the powerful instinctive force we sometimes ruefully know. But the better we understand it, the easier it is to avoid or deflect.

Because jealousy is so pervasive and troublesome, it was an early subject of study by experts in human behavior. Freud, Jung, and Adler made psychoanalytic studies focusing on jealousy's precise nature, cause, and role in personality development. Today most psychiatrists believe jealousy is an emotion universally experienced, initially in infancy.

Judging from their observations, they feel some experience with jealousy is an inevitable part of the maturation process.

The stage is set for this experience during a child's first year of life. The infant is totally dependent on others for the satisfaction of virtually all its needs, fulfilled in most cultures by its mother. To the infant the mother is unique and its love for her is possessive and demanding. Babies being what they are and social structures being what they are, the mother devotes a considerable amount of time attending to her infant's needs. By the end of the first year, the child has grown accustomed to the exclusive and unlimited possession of the mother's attention and love. However, at some point the mother usually becomes less attentive to her child, a change that the child invariably interprets as a threat. Up to now the mother has provided food, physical warmth, stroking, play. The baby is beginning to differentiate among these things, but all originate with the mother and still seem interconnected. As perceived by an infant, diversion of the mother's attention to someone or something else could seem like a threat to life itself. The manner in which a mother eases away from exclusive attention to the infant and how secure the baby has felt until that time probably will determine how vulnerable to jealousy it is as an adult.

Later, we may be jealous not only of a human rival but of a job or other activity that diverts a loved one's attention. We can understand jealousy of "things" if we recall an infant wanting, but not receiving, its mother's attention. The baby feels stricken by the apparent lack of attention. Whether that attention is going to another person or an activity is immaterial to the infant. What matters is that it's going away.

The immobilizing terror, the nameless horror (fear is too mild a term) described by some people in the throes of jealousy was probably experienced by them as infants

before conscious memory. Our experiences accummulate.
We measure the import of each against the total. Life is
first measured in seconds, then in minutes, later in years.
That is why attention is being redirected to a baby's first
moments outside the womb, why obstetricians now ponder
the effects of bright lights in the delivery room, the room
temperature, and the procedure of separating the baby
from its mother in a nursery.

Our earliest experiences are the most powerful, and
some of them will always influence our responses. Although
age allows us to accept some events tranquilly that earlier in
life caused distress, some emotionally charged circumstances
may produce an instantaneous, uncontrollable regression to
infantile fears. When asked at what age jealousy disappears,
a nineteenth-century French noblewoman replied, "I do
not know, I am only sixty-three."

The baby, inexplicably denied for the first time its
mother's breast-arm-face-voice, has no prior experience to
judge whether she will or will not return. It does not know
how to exist without her, and in fact cannot exist without
her. This is a baby with visceral pain, believing it is facing
death or an incomprehensible world. At its most basic
level, jealousy later in life is this fear of death. The feeling
of helplessness experienced by jealous people is often due
to an emotional reversion to a time when they were infants
and, in fact, helpless. Jealousy is intimately connected
with insecurity. Insecurity makes us more vulnerable to
jealousy, and jealousy is rooted in the ultimate insecurity—a
feeling that all that nurtures us is going or gone and may
never return.

At one to two years of age the child may become aware
that the mother's affection is being shared with the father.
If enough emotional security and independence have been
achieved, the child gracefully endures the transition to
shared love.

Quite often a child experiences jealousy following the birth of siblings. Once more the child may feel its emotional security threatened by a new competitor for the mother's affection—sometimes sensing a change even before the arrival of the competition.

A musician friend of mine, the second of three brothers, recalled an incident that occurred when he was four years old. "My mother was six months pregnant with my younger brother at the time. I was lying all warm and cozy next to her on the living room sofa when she decided to get up. I was angry that she wanted to do something else rather than be with me, so I socked her in the stomach. I didn't do it so much to hurt her as to hurt whoever, or whatever, was growing inside her. I felt that she wanted to get up because of what was growing inside her. She had to lie down for a few more minutes after that and I remember feeling very guilty."

An infant's reaction—crying and screaming—to perceived threats is protective. A baby's cry can express fear, grief, or rage. The noise attracts attention and perhaps food and stroking. Later in life a perceived threat may produce jealous reactions that are protective in intent but not in effect. How do you feel if you walk into a room and find your mate or date engaged in animated conversation with an attractive stranger, or perhaps an acquaintance or friend? Chances are, your reaction will largely depend on how you feel about *yourself* at the time. If you've just been complimented on your appearance, recently had praise for your work, feel physically fit, and are generally sure of your self-worth, a lot more provocation than idle party flirting is required to put you into a jealous rage.

On the other hand, if you've had an unfortunate childhood, which makes you particularly vulnerable to feelings of inadequacy (no blame, please—there is no formula for perfect child rearing), have lost your job, or suffer illnesses and the thought your body is betraying you, you're a prime candidate for fits of jealousy.

My study of jealousy began when I realized the emotion was occurring more frequently than it had at any other time in my past. Friends seemed surprised when I confided I was experiencing a lot of jealousy. "You, jealous?" they'd ask. After all, I was the one who advised others about their problems. What had changed, I asked myself. Not my childhood, and I was in good health. However, my work was in a state of flux at the time. Although I'd achieved some success with my Dr. Hip newspaper column, I thought I'd gone as far as I could in answering questions about sex and drugs. I wanted to write about a broader range of subjects. It seemed the only way out of the neat strongbox I'd constructed was to stop writing the column. But I hadn't realized how much it meant to me, how much my identity was commingled with the Dr. Hip character I'd created. For five years I stopped writing my regular newspaper medical column.

Two weeks before the last syndicated Dr. Hip column appeared, in July 1973, a moment's carelessness plunged me into the deepest anguish I had yet known. I was pulling out of a friend's driveway, making a left turn, when a motorcycle ran into the side of my car.

The moment is forever etched in my memory: a motorcycle carrying two people hurtling out of a blind turn, its driver futilely trying to stop; then the thud against the left side of my car. A young woman was hospitalized for five days as a result of the accident. During that time I was filled with feelings of guilt, remorse, and fear for her health and very life. A driver since the age of fourteen, I'd never before had an accident and was always proud of my driving skills. As a result of the accident, I was cited for a traffic violation.

I have never been conventionally religious, but for five

days and nights I prayed for the recovery of that young woman. It made no difference that the road involved is favored for racing by motorcyclists and sports-car drivers or that overgrown shrubbery blocked my view. The accident could have been avoided.

My self-confidence shattered, my column ended, I drifted into uncertainty. Unwarranted and unaccustomed jealousy was one of the most disturbing symptoms I experienced during this period of profound insecurity.

> Jealousy is one of those affective states, like grief, that may be described as normal. If anyone appears to be without it, the inference is justified that it has undergone severe repression and consequently plays all the greater part in his unconscious mental life. The instances of abnormally intense jealousy met with in analytic work reveal themselves as constructed of three layers. The three layers or stages of jealousy may be described as (1) competitive or normal; (2) projected; and (3) delusional jealousy.*
>
> —Sigmund Freud

Freud believed the pain of normal adult jealousy was really a reopening of old psychic wounds first sustained in infancy. In competitive or normal jealousy, one feels griefstricken over the loss or threatened loss of a loved one. Competitive jealousy is commonly experienced in social situations like parties, which often serve as ritual meeting grounds.

The second type of jealousy, projected jealousy, has two components: (1) fantasies of being unfaithful to one's partner or the experience of actual "unfaithfulness," and (2) the

*Freud: Dictionary of Psychoanalysis, New York: Philosophical Library, 1958.

need to rationalize urges regarded as unallowable or shameful. An individual struggling with guilt from real or fantasized infidelity may resolve this conflict by attributing these "sins" to his or her partner. The subconscious dialogue goes "I want to be with another person, but I can't accept this in myself. Therefore I accuse *you* of wanting another person." Or, "If I were my mate I'd make love to that person. Therefore she (he) must want to do the same." This process can be fairly complex, but the end result is accusing a lover of the very things one has perpetrated or fantasized. As someone once said, "A man does not look behind the door unless he has stood there himself."

This type of projection often explains extreme cases of jealousy. A New York psychologist remembers such an example:

"I was treating a woman who had suffered from her husband's pathological jealousy for several years. From the moment they married he would not permit her to do anything on her own. He wouldn't let her out of the house alone. He was suspicious of her phone calls. He was so prone to violence if she so much as looked at another man that they rarely went out to dinner or to social gatherings. Sometimes they would have violent arguments and he'd beat her. Finally, the issue exploded one night when they were at a bar and another man began talking to her. The husband slapped her. She was humiliated and furious. The police were called, at which point she lunged for a police officer's gun in an attempt to shoot her husband. They restrained her."

Unable to accept his own fantasies of wanting other lovers, the husband "gave" the fantasies to his wife, finding it easier to deal with strong suspicions that *she* wanted others. The therapist added that such occurrences were not unusual in his practice.

The third type of jealousy delineated by Freud—delusional—is the most extreme manifestation of this emotion. Delusional jealousy is based on clues that don't really exist, except in the victim's mind. Psychotic individuals may have this type of pathological jealousy as part of their disturbed thought processes.

Dr. Francis Rigney told of such a patient whose delusional jealousy was associated with a paranoid psychosis. His jealous rages often ended in his trying to strangle his wife; and two former wives had left him because of such incidents. The third was saved only by neighbors who heard her muffled screams and rushed into the house to intervene.

The psychiatrist gave these details: "This guy had somehow gotten the idea that his wife was having sexual relations in elevators with all the different Otis elevator repairmen in the city. He was absolutely convinced that she was regularly meeting her repairmen lovers in skyscraper elevators. He thought they'd push all the buttons to keep the elevator going up and down long enough for them to make love inside.

"The event that triggered the assault on his wife was a newspaper review of a novel about China entitled *The Green Dragon*. The patient had interpreted this review as an elaborate coded message from his wife to the Otis elevator repairmen, telling them to beware of the green-eyed monster [the husband] because he had discovered their secret. Whereupon the husband tried to strangle his wife before she had a chance to tell her elevator lovers the game was up."

Dr. Rigney continued: "I remember sending him to a psychologist for a Rorschach test. The psychologist hadn't been briefed on the case, so he had no idea what to expect from the patient. Well, he sent back the results and reported to me: "This man is a homicidal maniac. He saw blood on all ten cards, and as you may know, only three of the cards have any color on them.' He saw mutilated penises on every card—which is a hell of a sick response."

Paranoia is in part a reaction to insecurity, a defense mechanism gone haywire. The paranoid individual is not just ever-alert but over-alert, frequently making false connections and interpretations. Paranoids are over-alert to love rivals and inordinately jealous because they're desperately trying to defend against the insecurity the loss of a loved one represents. Like all jealous lovers, they graphically imagine sexual contact with the real or imagined love rival, but they're more frequently and more unreasonably jealous than most people because of their extreme insecurity and grossly disturbed thought processes.

"Crazy" people may experience a lot of jealousy, but you're not necessarily psychotic just because you feel jealous (though people in its grip have wondered about temporary insanity). Jealousy itself is no more abnormal than anger, grief, or joy. You're probably reading this because you or someone you know feels jealousy too intensely or too frequently. If you think these words are really a coded message to your lover, they may not help resolve your basic problem. Otherwise, you're on the path to understanding and controlling these perplexing feelings.

Among the therapists interviewed for this book was a prominent psychiatrist notably successful at dealing with sibling rivalry, my brother, Frank Schoenfeld, M.D. He finds that out-patients in therapy frequently complain about jealousy.

"It's a common problem. For example, a man has become involved with another woman and his wife feels jealous and won't know what to do about it. Or vice versa.

"One woman told me, 'I do mind him being involved, though it's not so bad if they go to her place or to a hotel room. But when I was away visiting my parents they used *our* bed in *our* house. And when I was vacuuming the rug and cleaning house I found these bobby pins.'

"Or just by chance they'll find an item of endearment. Usually it's a bit of shame they'll feel, especially if it's a question of entering into a private area like a bureau drawer. I guess what happens is—you understand, I don't get it straight from them—they'll get suspicious and then start looking for clues.

"A lot of interesting things happen in terms of these triads. Frequently the wife will get involved with the mistress. I've seen it go a number of ways. The wife might get very angry at the mistress but still continue the contact rather than cut it off. If she's in contact with the mistress there's a certain gratification that goes with that. A vicariousness. And sometimes it gets to the point where they become friends."

My brother thinks people in therapy usually don't experience the emotion purely, don't handle jealousy the way most people do. They tend to blame themselves rather than being angry with the other parties or doing something assertive about it. Instead of thinking they've been wronged, their jealous feelings seem a blow to self-esteem.

During acute jealousy episodes he helps them see the situation from a broader perspective. When the immediate crisis has passed, they explore ways to protect themselves in the future.

"It's really difficult at those times for them to separate feelings from objective fact, for people in the midst of a jealous funk to free themselves enough to work through these feelings.

"People who aren't ashamed to admit they're jealous, who describe it as a justified emotion, often describe it as love. They 'love the person so much,' that's why they're jealous. We explore it then from that aspect, trying to find out what's really going on—what is love and what is possessiveness.

"On the other hand, I've had people describe a situation involving jealousy and then deny they're jealous about it. One individual who comes to mind is a woman who had had numerous relationships with men, was married to a man much younger than herself, and was very controlling in their relationship. She had experienced everything that could be experienced. She'd been everywhere, she'd lived on communes, taken all kinds of drugs, gone through meditation, explored all kinds of relationships. She regarded herself as her husband's teacher. But then the time came when she started having relationships outside their marriage, and then he started seeing other women, too. She was really upset by that. But she absolutely denied the fact that she was jealous. She'd say, 'I'm not jealous, I'm just angry with him for going out with women who don't offer him anything: angry that he could go out with somebody who is such a comedown from me. How could he lower himself to somebody like that? I wouldn't mind if he went out with somebody who really had some class.''

My brother said denying jealousy in this manner is typical of people who fall into a "free life-style" model. "It used to be thought that to be jealous was un-Christian, that your love was not pure. Now if you're jealous, you're hung up, you're on an ego trip, you're unenlightened."

Most people are ashamed of their jealousy. When asked why, they'll say it's an immature emotion they should have outgrown. But these feelings are also produced by disturbing unconscious thoughts. Lovers merge with one another mentally as well as physically. The closer they become, the more strongly they identify with each other. It's as if the other person were an invisible Siamese twin.

My brother notes, "You've probably read that psychoanalysts feel that a lot of jealousy, and anger about it, is related to thoughts of sharing or being in the same place where another person of the same sex has recently been. That complaint comes up with some of my more open patients who will say something like, 'I didn't like him coming home from that other woman and putting his penis in me.' That kind of thing.''

It was early psychoanalysts who observed an association between paranoid jealousy and thoughts of sex with the rival, usually unconscious thoughts. Delusional jealousy in psychotics, they believed, was really a reaction to desire for sexual contact with members of the same sex. Material drawn from the unconscious, like the Rorschach test of the psychotic man in the Otis elevator case mentioned earlier, seemed to verify this idea. Noting the repeated association of delusional jealousy and thoughts of sex with the rival, psychoanalysts concluded this kind of jealousy was a reaction to desires that could not be consciously acknowledged. According to this theory, the thoughts of the Otis-elevator-case husband went something like "I want men, they want me. No, they don't. They want my wife.''

In fact, traditional psychoanalysts believe every instance of sexual jealousy includes a desire for the rival. It is one of those intriguing psychological concepts involving the idea that what's expressed consciously is the opposite of the true unconscious feeling.

At first, none of my research seemed to conflict with these psychoanalytic concepts. One woman guilelessly told me she dealt with her jealous feelings by imagining she was her boyfriend making love to her female rival! But a breach appears in these traditional theories when one examines some less traditional relationships.

What happens when jealousy arises in a situation where one's rival is of the opposite sex? Love triangles may be eternal, but today it has become almost commonplace for the rival to be the same sex as a lover or spouse. What then? Covert heterosexuality?

Perhaps what psychoanalysts have truly observed is that jealous lovers often do imagine sexuality between the love object and the rival. Since lovers identify with each other so strongly, a wandering lover carries the partner into a rival's bed like an invisible Siamese twin. The Siamese twin may be repelled by the situation, enjoy it, or be indifferent (though indifference is difficult in such close quarters). The reaction may be overt or covert, conscious or repressed. The rage of a jealous lover may be a reaction to shameful unconscious desires or a response to psychological rape. Whether or not the infidelity actually occurred or was merely suspected doesn't matter, in a sense. As in all matters of love, it's the thought that counts.

Psychoanalysts accurately noted the connection between jealousy and thoughts of sexual contact with the rival. They concluded, inaccurately, that these thoughts were all pleasurable, though usually unconscious. But this imagined sexual contact may be pleasurable or unpleasurable. Feelings of shame or anger associated with jealousy may be related to unconscious feelings of pleasure or feelings of being violated by the rival. The Siamese twin may be volitionless or may encourage the love object to wander into continuous adventures.

In other words, we are part of the people we love and they are part of us. A wandering lover, therefore, puts his or her partner in sexual contact with the rival.

Apart from theories of unconscious thoughts, there is no doubt many people find jealousy consciously disturbing. They experience a complex emotion in which the potential loss of a loved one to a third party can produce feelings of anger, fear, rejection, loneliness, betrayed trust, grief, despair, and loss of self-esteem. Vulnerability to jealousy is increased by feelings of inadequacy, whether basic to one's personality or produced by a specific life situation. This relationship of insecurity to jealousy is the key to understanding and finally mastering the emotion.

7   Groups, Gays, and Other Ways

One of the few previously published books wholly devoted to jealousy was written by a husband-and-wife team, Marguerite and Willard Beecher, and called *The Mark of Cain: An Anatomy of Jealousy.** The authors dedicate this rather Calvinistic book to their minister, truly treat jealousy as one of the seven deadly sins, and are convinced that jealousy is basic to all character disorders. Their God is apparently a wrathful God: "We can't prevent the jealous person from seeing the world through his bent and twisted spectacles, if he insists on having such a vision. That is his misfortune, and our efforts to placate him will only feed his desire for further assurance on our part. . . .''

Although it is never admitted, one wonders whether *The Mark of Cain*, like the original mark of Cain (and this book), developed as a response to jealousy. Writing about

*New York: Harper & Row, 1971

marriage, the Beechers say, "There is no such thing as a little jealousy."

They liken jealousy to a state of war: "the enemy sets the whole condition of our lives as long as we remain at war. . . . He becomes a complete obsession. The condition of a jealous person is all this and more. He is like a country occupied by the enemy. During the occupation he doesn't have his own law but a complete subservience to outside authority."

The Beechers are not alone in thinking that jealousy, like war, is hell. Among the more important reasons for recent social and sexual experimentation is an attempt to avoid the pain and difficulty of jealousy. To varying degrees group sex, communal living, and homosexuality all contain an element of breaking free of conventional life-styles in order to be liberated from the tyranny of jealousy.

One afternoon at a New York party celebrating the liaison of a rather jealous friend and his bride-to-be, I met Dan Greenburg, best known for *How to Be a Jewish Mother*, a masterpiece that should have earned him the Pulitzer Prize for comic literature. Dan is also known to millions of *Playboy* readers for a series of funny and perceptive articles on contemporary sex in America. When we met, he was apparently planning an article on sexual jealousy and we spent a long time discussing the subject. Actually, I spent most of that time convulsed with laughter at his quick wit. Six months later *Playboy* published Greenburg's "Take My Wife—Please," a saga about jealousy of another man's wife. The setting was Sandstone, an organization that conducted Gestalt-type sensitivity training workshops, but was best known for its espousal of group sex. Located at the time atop a mountain near Los Angeles, Sandstone featured fifteen acres of grounds, a large, ninety-four-degree indoor swimming pool, and many beds, and it discouraged clothing and encouraged sexual exploration.

"Take My Wife—Please" describes Dan Greenburg's second visit to Sandstone, accompanied by a woman named Dianne and her husband, Bill. In the article, Greenburg remarks that it's too bad Sandstone is about to fold, since he'll therefore never have a chance to be there with a "primary" relationship and work through his jealousy when she has sex with another man. But reflecting on this he says, "Having a woman of mine make it with another guy and working through my jealousy about it are right there on my list of things to do after going sky diving with a pillowcase." Meanwhile, Greenburg is not only making love with Dianne but seemingly falling in love with her as well. When he learns she's had sex with someone else (other than her husband) Greenburg realizes he is jealous:

> What I am feeling is ridiculous. Listen, I tell myself, if you can put what you are feeling into a sentence, you will see how foolish this is and you will stop it. I put it into a sentence. The sentence is this: Bill's Wife Is Being Unfaithful To Me. It is funny. It doesn't make me laugh.

Still perplexed by his feelings, Dan later asks Dianne's husband if he ever gets jealous. Bill replies that he only experiences *time* jealousy. For example, if they have plans for a special holiday and she changes her plans to be with someone else, "*then* I might feel a little bad, yeah. But, otherwise, I love her enough to want her to be happy and do whatever it is that turns her on."

Sex with other lovers need not threaten a primary relationship and is not necessarily associated with the fear and feeling of loss that provokes jealousy. Jealousy will not appear, given two conditions:

1. If sex with others is not connected with feelings of losing the person and the relationship;

2. If indirect sexual contact with the third party, through the person of the loved one, does not produce thoughts of shame or guilt.

During the latter years of Sandstone, attendance at one or more Gestalt-type seminars was usually necessary before admission to the beds and other facilities. One of the earliest residents, a woman I'll call Molly, moved there in 1970 with her husband because they both wanted sex outside their marriage. "One of the reasons I liked Sandstone in 1970," she said, "was that it was a sink-or-swim type of environment. You could wear clothes or not—you could fuck if you wanted to and nobody was preparing you by talking about it first. Obviously there were discussions along with it, but they weren't organized. Now they send me these things in the mail—all these *groups*!"

Molly was "very nervous" when she and her husband first arrived at Sandstone. The first night there they started making love in the main room to catcalls from the others present. "You can't get it on with your own wife," the Sandstone residents teased. Her husband had sex with another woman that first night. "But it didn't bother me much because, in the first place, I felt support from her. It was out in the open. It wasn't like they snuck off and he didn't show up for two days or something like that. After they finished, Marty came back to me and was feeling really good. It was sort of an immediate reconfirmation of the fact that he was there with me.

"It took me a couple of nights. The first person I was with was very comfortable with it. I remember coming back into the main room afterwards and this man had his arm around me. We weren't wearing any clothes and we had obviously just been making love. But my husband just came up to me and gave me a big hug. And somehow it was a very natural kind of thing. Circumstances really help. Sandstone was a really good place to get that kind of support."

Molly observed that in a situation of nearly free sexuality, men were often more jealous than women, especially, and ironically, "the men who dragged their wives or girl friends there. I think it put a lot more pressure on the men than the women. Men have the added difficulty of trying to get it up in a strange situation.

"A man might be in the can or something and all of a sudden the woman would be gone. She could do anything. I mean, if she wanted to she could just have the men line up. I have a friend who did this. She said she's always wanted to be gang-raped and as close as she could come was just telling everybody in the place she wanted to do it. She gave everybody a number, like in a bakery."

Molly recalled intense jealousy only once at Sandstone, when she observed her husband and another woman walking on the grounds *holding hands*. "I'd seen him having sex with her lots of times, but there was something about his walking hand in hand with her up the hill." It was the intimacy.

Molly finally left Sandstone after one and a half years.

"It got to the point where there were three orgies a week—I couldn't stand the smell of sex. I didn't want it. I didn't want to see people fucking. I didn't want the bombardment of new people any more. I met somebody. I fell in love."

Molly's emotional involvement with a person outside the small group then living at Sandstone caused her to leave under duress. "They wouldn't let me back on the grounds again. I had smashed the ideal. I think the sin was we had a successful group marriage going and essentially I made the institution fall apart. At the time only four of us were really living there. I had abandoned the dream."

When I interviewed Molly, monogamous relationships

for her were "not even an alternative anymore." She was just ending a relationship with two men that had lasted for eighteen months. "It started with me loving one man and then loving another. And then it being all right for me to love both of them. One of them moved in, then the other moved into the house, so we were all living together. In that time I was also going to have a baby. Was trying to get pregnant. Wanted to get pregnant—with both of them. Many long discussions. Everybody thought it was a *great* idea. We were really excited about it. I got a tubal pregnancy right away. Took about a month, quite a while, to recover from that. It's a serious operation—I hadn't realized that before."

Complex emotional relationships can make a difficult emotion even more intricate. I asked Molly if the two men in her life were ever jealous of each other. "Only once," she replied. "One of them confessed to me, 'You know what got me really jealous? It was when you were jealous of him but you weren't jealous of me!' "

Their three-way relationship cracked when one of the men fell in love with another woman. Molly experienced an emotion she had almost forgotten.

"He fell in love and excluded me, both sexually and emotionally. I couldn't believe it. I hadn't felt like that in many years, wondering, Why do I feel like this? Why do I want to kill these people? Totally rejected and depressed. Consequently I got mad at them, and then after I left, I got mad at myself. But I felt the reasons for my jealousy were valid. In other words, it didn't seem sane to me not to be jealous in that situation."

Shut out as she was by one of her lovers, Molly's jealousy was rational, given the bounds the three had established. She hardly ever was jealous of the second man in her life, even though he frequently brought home other women. She explained why she was jealous of one of her lovers but not the other. "With one of them I never had the feeling he might not ever come back. Whether you know, trust, and like the other woman is very important, too. It's really difficult sometimes. It's the idea of—would you want your lover to fuck your friends or your enemies?

"When people feel threatened, the question is whether it's a falsely perceived threat or a real threat, and if it's a real threat, what are you going to do about it? If it's a falsely perceived threat you might as well get rid of it, because otherwise it will make the real threat more likely."

When one of the two men in her life fell in love with another woman Molly correctly identified the situation as a real threat.

The following vignette illustrates why jealousy need not arise when a true threat is impossible. It was contributed by a well-known musician who wishes to remain anonymous:

"A few years ago I was traveling in Europe and learned a woman friend was living near a small village in Northern Italy. Karen was a beautiful, intelligent woman who had been married to one of my friends. Their marriage had broken up—partly due to jealousy, I think—and she began living with Matt, whose occupation at the time was cocaine smuggling. Karen had become involved as a runner or courier. They were arrested in a state with severe penalties for drug sales and faced long prison terms if convicted. The prosecutor had a good case against them but promised leniency if they would inform on and 'set up' other drug smugglers. Once freed on bail, they looked at their options and fled the country.

"Now they lived in Europe, two among many Americans exiled because of drug-law violations. Fearful of extradition, they never lived in one place for very long, but I learned their location from another trusted friend and, after a series of telephone calls, arranged to visit them.

"Karen and Matt lived in a small apartment on the second floor of what had been a storage building on a farm. They lived quietly, had little contact with their former world, and were glad to see me. For several days I filled them in on news from the United States and what their friends were doing. I had always found Karen attractive, felt love for her really, but never expressed these feelings physically, and only indirectly, verbally.

"One evening Matt, Karen, and I went to Milan to see *Last Tango in Paris*. When we returned, the three of us wound up making love together. It certainly wasn't the movie—I just turned on to Karen. The next day was Easter Sunday, a beautiful spring day which we spent lying out in the sun. The night before, I'd had fantasies of going away with Karen. Realistically though, this was impossible, even if she had wanted the same thing—because she was a fugitive and couldn't return to the United States. But my fantasy-wish had created some tension between Matt and me, felt initially by me. I decided to leave the following day, two days earlier than planned.

"When it was time to go I gave Matt a 'brother' hug and kissed Karen. Our kiss became kisses and almost without our knowing it we kneeled and then lay down on a rug before the fireplace. We began making love. The quality of our lovemaking was made special by the knowledge we would see each other again only by chance, or perhaps never. All this time Matt was sitting beside us playing his guitar. He was playing his guitar, in fact *for us*, in some kind of fantastic escalation of the more common, but always lovely, ceremony of musicians singing for lovers. He even improvised his song, ending with a soft, sweet, and sincerely friendly 'Good-bye my friend, good-bye my friend' as Karen and I lay in each other's arms, feeling time slip away from us. They drove me to the train station and we made tentative plans to meet later in Sicily to watch a solar eclipse. But I never saw them again.''

Marin County, California, was the subject of an hour-long 1978 study by NBC television called ''I Want It All Now.'' The resulting documentary depicted a community of wealthy people eager to try any social encounter while immersed in hot tubs and stroked by peacock feathers. Although the television program exaggerated matters, it is true that the human-potential movement in its many forms does thrive in the bedroom communities across the Golden Gate Bridge from San Francisco. Marinites have experimented with ''open marriage'' for at least the last thirty years.

One of the couples interviewed for this book were friends and students of Alan Watts. Ed and Maggie had just celebrated their thirty-sixth wedding anniversary.

Maggie: Where do we start? When we were kids we were together for about a year and then the war came along. Ed went away for four years, during which time we behaved as though we were single. Then we lived together again, and have been together since.

Ed: At one stage we were very much into an open-marriage sort of thing. And our best friend and Maggie decided they wanted to make a scene together. It was thoroughly agreeable. We all knew and loved each other. It was great. It was all arranged and set up. But when it happened, I flipped, totally absolutely completely went off my goddamn rocker. Sat in front of a fire for three days and wouldn't talk to anybody. And I got sick and the whole schmeer. It was such an intense emotional trip that either I survived the whole thing and came through it or else I died. It was that kind of an either/or scene. As far as I'm concerned, that was the trial by fire, just absolute. To live in that state of jealousy, to experience that kind of emotion, is incompatible with existence.

Maggie: You almost killed me.

Ed: Yeah, it almost killed me, too. I was totally and completely out of it. It went its course, did its number, and I recovered. And I have never been anywhere near to experiencing that sort of thing again.

Maggie and Ed subsequently conducted a less open marriage. Maggie was always wary of Ed's feelings from that time on.

Ed: But you and Paul later made it, and that was cool.

Maggie: I never trusted you, though. Didn't know if you were going to flip out. Whenever you said it was okay, I wasn't sure whether you meant it or not. Like at that party at Rita's place, where the guy I went off with . . . you put me down on a level of "he wasn't good enough" somehow.

Ed: Exactly. He was a noplace guy.

Maggie: But I think that's another ego thing.

Ed: It wasn't jealousy. At least not the way I experience jealousy.

Ed was thinking of the intense depression and grief experienced when his wife left with their best friend. We cannot know his unconscious feelings when Maggie went off with the "noplace guy" at Rita's place. If you recall the Siamese-twin theory of jealousy discussed earlier, perhaps Ed identified with a bedmate he found unattractive. Since these unconscious trysts with rivals of the same sex may be morally and psychologically unacceptable, Ed could have expressed the same disdain whether he thought the fellow was "noplace" or really a winner.

Maggie: Well, in recent years the story has been very
    different. I have total freedom now [laughs]. I'm
    fifty-seven, and I don't have the same figure, and the
    line isn't forming to the right. I've got all the freedom
    in the world.

I'm very jealous. I rarely am able to really accept
Ed's involvement with other women, regardless of
whether he sleeps with them or not. And they're
generally my women friends. This is very hard for
me.

It's the panic of, they're younger and more attractive,
which is my own insecurity. I get in a real bad place,
and I don't handle it well. That's who I am. It isn't
ideal and I'm not proud of it. But that's how it is.

I can't change him. He's still free to do whatever he
wants. All I can do is say I won't live with him if that
situation is present. Because I lose his attention, his
interest. There are no goodies in it for me. Mostly
there's the fear of losing him. Plus, I usually lose my
woman friend, too, because the thing gets sticky and
either they're uncomfortable with Ed's interest, or
they're more interested in him than me, whatever,
and the friendship is dissolved. So that's where we
are right now. I don't know about tomorrow.

Ed was asked whether he had ever found a way to
prevent or relieve Maggie's jealousy when he was involved
with another woman. He admitted he'd never been able to
assuage his wife's fears.

Maggie: Surely we can love more than one person at a
    time. But when I'm really fascinated by a man, that's
    where I am. My thoughts are there, my attention is
    there. And it isn't that I'm not thinking of Ed, it's just
    that my consciousness is someplace else. So this
    business of ''there's lots to go around and nobody is

really missing anything'' is, I think, a pile of hokum. Certainly when you're involved with somebody else, your attention is with him.

But Maggie seemed ambivalent on the issue of open marriage. Her fears frequently dealt with her age.

Maggie: If I were in my twenties or thirties or even forties again, I could be busy with somebody else. Like Kathy and Richard. They've really got an open marriage, but there are goodies going all around and no one feels left out.

Ed: You feel left out?

Maggie: Oh, sure I do!

One Sunday evening while the late Alan Watts was doing his regular radio program, he spoke directly to his group of friends, including Maggie and Ed. ''You're not as free as you think you are,'' Watts said. ''You're getting into a lot of trouble.''

Maggie: We got into, y'know, Zen. And everybody in our little group was playing musical beds. Our freedom was a concept—it wasn't coming from a true feeling. I mean, we're all products of our environment, and we were all getting into a mess—everybody we knew. And Ed and I and this one other couple are the only ones who stayed together. The others have split many times over.

As they near their sixties, Ed and Maggie still haven't completely resolved their attitudes toward open marriage. A few months before they were interviewed, Ed had a fling with another of Maggie's friends. When Maggie objected, her woman friend was miffed. ''She gave me hell,'' Maggie said, ''because I wouldn't share my husband. I asked Ed, 'Where are your priorities, there or here?' ''

Ed: They were here, of course! There's just something about going away and coming back with new energy to share with you. . . .

Maggie: I'll tell you when I can go along with it. When the other woman is married or living with a man she really cares about. Then I don't really feel that threatened. If it's just an interlude, then I can accept it. But when she's solo, younger, and available, and more attractive . . .

I would guess Ed and Maggie will continue this dialogue as long as they are married. I also suspect they'll remain married as long as they live.

The book *Getting Clear** is a collection of personal growth experiences and interviews by Ann Kent Rush, a prominent feminist author. Part of the book deals with jealousy and the work of Lynn Smith (who, with sociologist Gordon Clanton, subsequently edited *Jealousy,* an anthology of writings on jealousy). When interviewed by Ann Kent Rush, Lynn Smith had recently completed a study of couples exploring forms of sexual freedom. She recommended that couples share with their partners their sexual feelings about others, and openly ask questons about a partner's attraction or actual involvement with someone else. Smith suggested couples considering opening their relationship to others ask themselves questions like: If you believe someone can love only one person at a time, does this mean a partner having outside sex doesn't love you? Do you think a partner's attraction to someone else implies you are sexually inadequate? Do you think you're not meeting your partner's needs? Do you think jealousy is a measure of love? If your partner doesn't get jealous, do you think he or she doesn't care?

*New York: Random House, 1973.

How secure or insecure do you feel together? How satisfied are you together? Dissatisfied? Dependent on each other? Do you wish to see others because things between you are bad, or because you feel happy and open? How committed are you to keeping the primary relationship going, no matter what else is happening?

She suggested couples make agreements between themselves that may be changed. For example, letting your partner know what you wish to do before you act, or "not too often" or "only if I like the other person." The agreement might specify that it's all right for one partner to have outside sex only if the other is similarly involved. Some couples may choose to do everything (and everyone) together, with no separate outside dates. Others do what they like when the partner is out of town. Some couples get involved only with people who have other primary relationships, discouraging emotional involvements by having "just sex." Smith believes each new relationship must have an initial monogamous period for the new mates. If things are good at home, she states, you've got the edge on anybody else.

She gave further advice for couples wishing an open relationship:

1. Outside people should know you and your partner have an open relationship.
2. Let the other person know he or she is not viewed as a rival.
3. Allow no difference between what you and your partner tell each other, and what the other person is told about the relationship.
4. The three of you can spend time together. This reduces the chances of feeling lonely, "left out," or fearful of the unknown. You can thus compare reality with fantasies about the other person.

5. Discuss the question of whether it's possible and comfortable for the three of you to have sex together.

Lynn Smith suggested two surprising benefits of open relationships. One is renewed sexual interest at home. Another may be a couple's finding that the grass is not necessarily greener on the other side.

Gays and Jealousy

Emotional security is often tenuous among members of minorities living in a larger society. A minority status regarded with hostility and fear by the larger society—whether racial, sexual, economic, or religious—may render even more difficult the task of achieving and maintaining individual emotional security. But many gays, including some gay therapists, maintain that their life-style greatly reduces jealousy. Do gays experience jealousy differently from straights? Are they more or less jealous than heterosexuals?

In the large homosexual communities that flourish in cities like San Francisco, New York, and Los Angeles, some gay men and lesbian women have attempted to avoid traditional heterosexual role models in their relationships. These departures from traditional norms might be expected to affect the role of jealousy in their lives.

Harry is a writer in his late thirties who "came out" several years ago. When I first met him at an artist's party in San Francisco, Harry was wearing a winged silver lamé costume and performing an exotic dance. He proved to be an articulate and enthusiastic supporter of the gay life. Though he admitted jealousy existed in any community, he began his interview by maintaining, "Our freedom to experiment has made jealousy easier to deal with. In a real sense we have rejected the heterosexual world, something the politicization of gays has accomplished. Prior to this time there was the attempt to emulate the straight tradition—the man-and-wife models—but it was obvious that eventually the questions of who would do the dishes and who would change the tire were pathetic and absurd. So eventually a new point of view developed along the lines of: 'We've been oppressed by the male chauvinist pig, want nothing to do with him, he's screwed up, his women are screwed up. And here we are with a wonderful opportunity to explore what we are. We have this different kind of sexuality. What's it all about?' "

But Harry's way of avoiding jealousy seemed to be by maintaining distance, avoiding emotional dependency, a method also common to many straight people. "I've been jealous from time to time," he said. "I think jealousy starts to occur when you have relationships. When you care. I've had very few relationships. I've had many difficulties with my gayness for many years, and the first time I really cut free was when I lived in Morocco. I started to have relationships with Arab boys. The equalities were very strange because I was the master, I was in charge, I had the money.

"I was with a poor Tangier boy who needed the money and was very happy to be my servant, in a way. He was very happy to do anything I said and to sleep with me and have sex with me. He enjoyed that. But I was in control in almost every sense. We were very affectionate, and I could ask him to spend the night and he would, and then I could ask him to leave the next day when I had work to do and see him again in a couple of days.

"I became very attached to him and began wondering, What does he do when we're not together? I started to ask a few questions—do you have other lovers? I would never get a satisfactory answer. There would be a laugh or a smile or an evasion. Sometimes I would get a story that I'd realize had nothing to do with the truth. I learned not to ask these questions and I realized how foolish it was, because when the boy was with me the relationship was total, perfect. There was no question of anybody else. It was absurd to be jealous in this situation.

"I was in love, I suppose, with this boy. The relationship went on for several months, and I was jealous on several occasions."

Harry now retreated a bit from the notion that a homosexual life-style made jealousy easier to deal with.

"I would think that qualitatively there is no difference." But he maintained that the easy sexuality in gay communities did reduce the number of jealous episodes experienced. I asked him how this new sexual freedom made it easier to deal with jealousy.

"Well, I think jealousy arises out of restrictions. In a gay community where you can have multiple relationships, jealousy may be less of a problem. There's an openness to the idea of friendships with many people, which may include sex. For one thing, if you lose a lover you needn't fear remaining alone for long. You have the feeling there will always be someone else. There's less emphasis on the importance of long-term bonding. These differences from straight values seem to reduce jealousy."

But is this really different from jealousy-avoidance techniques used by many straight people? If one doesn't care deeply for other people, jealousy will certainly be reduced. Multiple brief sexual encounters have always been characteristic of many male homosexuals. Could it be that Harry had cause and effect reversed? Perhaps the pattern of frequent brief sexual encounters seen in so many male homosexuals originates, in part, as a defense against the pain of jealousy.

A New York graphic designer described an aspect of the sexual cornucopia available in most large gay communities: "The baths are where a lot of it happens. You're basically there only for sex. You're nude, everything's literally out front, and anonymity allows you to have the kind of sexual adventure and fantasy fulfillment you can't get otherwise, without becoming involved in some kind of relationship. The place I go to occasionally has a hot pool and a walk-through maze for sexual activities. There are private stalls for those who want them, with doors and beds. Upstairs, there's a lounge with a forty-eight-inch TV set which plays porno video cassettes. They run for about twenty minutes, then stop for about fifteen while all the lights go out. Obviously it's designed for totally anonymous, totally faceless sex. It's not the kind of place where you're going to find people feeling jealous."

The availability of this kind of experience can be both a threat and a safety valve to gay relationships. "I was really upset when Phil told me he'd gone to the baths," said a television producer who'd been living with his partner three years. "It happened about a year ago when we weren't getting along very well and were sexually bored. But after I cooled down I realized it would have been more serious if he'd gone bar-hopping looking for sex and maybe a new relationship. *That* would have made me really jealous and angry."

A gay photographer sees an advantage to having the bath, bar, and disco scenes all available: "I think it's healthy because it allows you to control the degree of your involvement—or noninvolvement—to suit your needs. I'm not regularly into any of those scenes, but there are times when it's so good to just jump into the craziness of the baths and get it on with some guy whose name I don't know and whom I'll never see again. I will admit sometimes being jealous when my lover goes to the baths, but that feeling passes. The occasional night out is something we allow each other without really talking about it.''

A therapist who leads a weekly encounter group for gay men discussed his group's feeling about having a night out. ''There's very little support for it. The group's attitude is, 'You want one night out a week, live by yourself. You want a monogamous trip? Fine, live with a person.' It's a conservative feeling, quite definitely, but I'm sure it's because there are a lot of people in the group who've been burned badly in past relationships.''

A former Catholic priest who came out of the cloister says, ''There are aspects of the gay life-style that militate against long-term relationships. The traditional man and wife roles are nonexistent, no children will be raised, and there are no social pressures to bolster a commitment in a relationship. Plus there are a lot of opportunities to get involved in casual sex, which can cause jealousy when a relationship exists. It's difficult to generalize but I sense that gays are almost forced by circumstance to find new ways of living together, more so than straights.''

Cynthia, an attractive restaurant manager in her late twenties who has lived for some years in San Francisco's Castro district and has a number of gay male friends, recalls a familiar variation on the jealousy game: ''Several times I've been caught in the middle of a situation like one which happened last week. Two friends, Jeffrey and Mark, invited me for dinner and both of them started flirting with me! It wasn't an attempt to engineer a three-way scene. They were just trying to make each other jealous. It was also obvious that either of them would sleep with a woman if the chemistry were happening. I think that's true with most of my gay friends—they're basically bisexual but choose to be homosexual, so there's always that potential."

Holly Woodlawn was one of Andy Warhol's discoveries and he starred in several of Warhol's films. When I interviewed him, his eyes were outlined by green make-up, though he was wearing blue jeans and a football jersey.

"When I get jealous I get hysterical. I'm half Puerto Rican and half German, so either way I have no choice. I'm either fire or ice.

"One day my lover and I went to a party and we had a wonderful time. We got drunk—that helped later events that evening a lot! Somehow we had this raging fight in the middle of the street. I thought he was doing something at the party he wasn't really doing, and he thought the same of me.

"Then the punches, black eyes, teeth. The next day he looked like a raccoon. Awful. He got up and went back to his parents.

"I'm sure the weather helps, too. In the middle of June on a very hot and muggy day I was walking down Twenty-second Street in Chelsea. Very nice and very English and trees. But there's like a little tiny three- or four-block area where there are Puerto Ricans. My pianist lives there, and I go there to rehearse. I had to walk half a block to the house, and I could just hear the groans going. I could feel it. . . . I saw a girl chasing her boyfriend with a machete, down the street in New York City, in 1976."

I asked Holly which would be worse in terms of jealousy: if the man he was with got involved with another man or with a woman.

"I think a man would be worse."

Are gay men more jealous than gay women? Ann, a

lesbian therapist who counsels gays of both sexes at a New York clinic, gives a qualified yes. "Gay men talk more about jealous feelings than lesbians. A lot of their jealousy seems to be centered around sexual activity. Perhaps they're just less inhibited about the subject of jealousy. Gay men may be saying more of what everybody else is only thinking—being bitchy rather than just pretending. But I do think lesbians would say that gay men and heterosexuals have more problems with jealousy than gay women.

"I think with gay men there's a greater emphasis on sex and less on other aspects of a relationship. They are seemingly able to divorce a portion of themselves for a time and go off and interact sexually with someone else, a stranger maybe. I'm not putting any judgment on that. For many, it means they are no longer denying themselves sexually. But women have always been allowed to be warmer and more caring than men. There doesn't seem to be the kind of jealousy in lesbian or straight women that there is in the gay and heterosexual male world."

What kind of jealousy crops up most frequently among lesbian women?

"It centers a lot around security—family involvements, job status, and other economic considerations. But I've also noticed that if a couple has an agreement about being monogamous and one of the partners wants to change that to be sexually free with others, no matter what escape clauses are contained in the agreement, it seems the other partner always ends up being jealous. She'll say 'I'm really hurt, I'm confused. I don't know what to do. I feel like I shouldn't be reacting, but I am.'

"There's been a tremendous amount of pressure—I think coming from the left in the women's community—to be nonmonogamous. So many people operated under the assumption they had to be sexually open to many people. And if they weren't, then something was wrong with them! But now sexual freedom is beginning to be regarded as just the opposite—the freedom *not* to be sexual. Many women who are monogamous feel that, the way our culture is now, the only way to offer security is to be monogamous. Actually, a lot of women feel freer to develop closeness to other women precisely because they are monogamous. Probably these women tend not to get as jealous over intimacy since the immediate connection is not sexual activity.''

But nonsexual jealousy can certainly be just as hard and heavy as sexual jealousy. Joy, a graduate student and a ''lesbian by choice,'' remembers what happened with two of her friends, Phyllis and Karen, both in their twenties:

''Phyllis had identified herself as a lesbian for a long time, but Karen was in the middle of the coming-out phenomenon—she still had many straight friends and was afraid she'd lose them were she to openly acknowledge her new relationship. The first clash came when Karen was invited to a party and tried to subtly suggest that Phyllis dress in feminine clothes to avoid offending her straight friends. Phyllis yelled, 'What? You want me to go back into the closet? To bring out the clothes that I keep for job interviews?'

''Phyllis was really hurt, but not as much as she'd be the following Christmas, which Karen said she would spend with her family, meaning her mother and father and sisters. Phyllis had been relating to the two of *them* as a family. When Karen left for a week in New Orleans, Phyllis saw it as a denial of their relationship. She was really jealous and angry.''

When one partner in a same-sex relationship feels a need for secrecy while the other wants to stand up and tackle the consequences, the situation is ripe for jealousy.

How to deal with a homosexual green-eyed monster? Stephanie, an articulate woman in her early thirties, lives in Chicago and has "been a lesbian since the age of four."

"I'm monogamous in my relationship," she says, "and have been for three years. But jealousy has been a concern. It's come up a number of times. Jane and I encourage each other to have other friends. And when you have friends and develop warm, intimate kinds of feelings, certainly sexual feelings are also going to come into play. In fact it's hard to imagine having a friend I don't have any sexual feelings for. But I've made a decision not to have actual sex with anyone else but Jane. I just happen to think it's difficult to hold together the kind of relationship we want and still be making it with another person. Recently someone has come along who Jane feels wants to snatch me away— which is not how I see it at all. So some jealousy has arisen."

How was it handled?

"I was really up front with both of them. I spoke with the other woman and made it clear I didn't want to have a sexual relationship with her. And I told Jane that her suspicions are completely unfounded. She'll just have to trust me. On the other hand, I know I can't love her jealousy away for her. All I can really do is reassure her and ask her to see how good our relationship is and how much I care for her. Beyond that she has to deal with her jealousy on her own."

And what happens when the tables are turned?

Stephanie continued, "Right. No matter how much trust is built up, there are times when I feel threatened. When that happens, I want to talk about it, share the pain. I don't want to carry it around. I always approach Jane when I feel storm clouds gathering. And yet I guess I'd be scared if I thought there wasn't anyone else who found her attractive.''

Jealousy may or may not be more common among homosexual men and women, but it clearly seems a factor in all human life regardless of sexual orientation. A gay life-style precludes jealousy only when no emotional attachments are formed.

8 Communing with Jealousy

In 1971 there were an estimated one to three thousand communes throughout the United States. One reason for their initial popularity was the belief that the communal life could virtually eliminate feelings such as anger, depression, envy, and jealousy.

A number of former and present commune residents were interviewed on the subject of jealousy. Some were residents of populous, widely publicized communes, while others lived quietly in remote areas, quasi-families numbering fewer than a dozen people. Most of them have long since returned to more conventional living arrangements.

The Wheeler Ranch, located in Sonoma County, California, on three hundred acres of rolling hills, attracted thousands of visitors as one of the best-known New Age communes. After several years of inactivity, the Wheeler Ranch is functioning again, but at a more subdued level. The owner of the ranch, Bill Wheeler, invited me to visit his commune and talk about jealousy.

Those allowed entry through the locked gate drive down a narrow road that soon swings sharply right and becomes a bumpy, unpaved wide trail. Along the way I gave a ride to two young women carrying groceries in boxes on their heads. They'd just arrived at the ranch from Florida and had hitched to town for provisions. After several hundred yards I dropped them off and they disappeared into the woods. The road leveled out and came to an end near some sheds and a large, freshly planted garden.

Bill Wheeler, scion of a wealthy Eastern manufacturing family, is a tall man in his mid-thirties with long blond hair and a full beard. He pointed out the garden patch where his daughter Raspberry was born and led me to a ramshackle trailer where he lived while a county-approved house awaited completion nearby. We dined simply, on vegetables grown at the ranch, with six of the current commune members. They left after supper and Wheeler described his experiences as *patron* of a world-famous and (to the neighbors) notorious commune.

"Our commune was not organized. We were more an R and R camp. They were very few group marriages and they didn't last very long. But we had just about every sexual trip happen at one time or another. I was in a position not many men have in their lives, being able to work through a lot of sexual fantasies. The relationships I was having with the women on the land were pretty casual. Like, 'Oh boy, there's a little fox. Yummy little thing, and I just want to lick that up and down.' And I did.

"Well, I had an old lady. During that time she got pregnant, and she had a child. And it seemed like during that time I was getting increasingly promiscuous. Unfortunately, I wasn't able to be honest with her about it. And when the first case of crabs came along, it was very difficult to explain to her how I got them, and how she got them. She sort of quasi-grew to accept that, but she was very bitter about the fact that I couldn't be honest with her about it. Never could be, partially for fear of losing her. A fear that she would start getting it on with other guys.

"Somehow when a man has a child by a woman, it raises the ante a lot. That's when jealousy rises to the level of 'Bang, you're dead.' I brought home this girl one time and we all slept together. To me it was pure ecstasy, but for the two women it was like hell because they were both in love with me, and neither wanted to share me. In fact, at the end of the night one of them said, 'I don't love you anymore.' And she was serious.

"My old lady fell in love with someone else—a friend! I went away, and it really took me about a year to get over it. And about two years to accept him as a friend again. Now we're just super close. I see now that he was making a woman happy whom I couldn't make happy.

"I'm able to feel my emotions better now. Before, they'd just bore inside and I'd be unhappy and brooding. When I get jealous now I throw myself into some kind of project. Or go on a trip. Going to the hot springs is my favorite, 'cause I really feel like a divine presence is there.

"I think a sexual dialogue with another person takes a lot of work and concentration. If you're getting it on with other people you can't really concentrate on your partner. Also, if you are really sexually happy and compatible, you really don't want to get it on with another. It's enough with one person. There's no reason why it shouldn't go on indefinitely. But it's so rare.

"I don't know, with all the sexual experimentation that went on, it all comes down to: you gotta be faithful to your old lady. If you're not faithful, you've got to be absolutely brutally honest with each other. That can work."

*   *   *

Gale lived at the Wheeler Ranch for several years. She's a small woman in her late twenties, with a nine-year-old daughter. Lounging in the comfortable living room of her cozy home, she remarked, "I'm getting more and more to enjoy being alone. Living at the ranch was the beginning of *my* study of jealousy. We all had to deal with it because about all people were doing there was getting stoned, playing music, and relating to each other. The atmosphere of the place was really open. You'd go to milk the cows at night and you'd find out who was doing what to whom.

"Twenty of us moved into a large ranch house. Everyone liked each other very much, and naturally we wanted to get as close to one another as we could. First my own experience was disillusionment, because I had a romantic idea of love. When the man I was with developed other relationships, I really had a feeling of failure. Jealousy was definitely a part of that. I felt bad for a while, then thought about why I was feeling that way. That's what led me to the next step, accepting that faithfulness was to love someone and be good enough friends to appreciate his other interests. But it took a lot of practice. At that time I got into bisexuality. I did it with a friend of mine, a very true-hearted wonderful person. It helped us understand what the other woman was feeling."

Another woman recounted her experiences on a commune in New Mexico:

"I remember going through that listening number. It was usually in the same bed. If I had room in my bed on a really cold night, it would be very rude not to share it with somebody. For a while I was having a relationship with a man and another woman, and on some nights there'd be the problem of the three of us lying there, with him in the middle. Now none of us would have talked openly about it, like, 'Are you going to get it on tonight, and which one of us are you going to get it on with?' Maybe nobody would get it on with anybody. But you knew who'd gotten it on last, and who might be horny.

"When I lived with two guys, only one of whom I was attracted to, what we ended up doing was waiting until the other one got up early to do the milking and then get it on *madly* while he was gone. We'd be resting when he got back!"

Some communes welcomed visitors, others didn't. A former resident of Hawaii described the price unsuspecting visitors might pay for an open commune policy.

"I lived in this place in the jungle on the Big Island. It was basically a long gigantic bed under a coconut palm frond roof where anybody could sleep and do what they wanted to. It was totally open. If you felt like it you could make love to whoever was lying next to you, but sometimes you *didn't* feel like making it with the person next to you—and if that person did, there was no easy way out. So heavy scenes went down all the time, particularly with visitors who would be very blown out by it all. There was one night when this guy realized his woman was sleeping with one of the people that lived with us. He was drunk and went into an incredible jealous rage and just started beating people, throwing them down on the rocks and screaming. Everyone was yelling and all the neighbors came running over. He was in extreme pain. The cries that came from his mouth. . . . I've never heard anything like it. He was a total animal."

It would be difficult to find a more touching tale of devotion to the new unconsciousness than the story of Lamar Jean, formerly of Frankfort, Kentucky.

"Back then my approach was: 'Love everybody and share what you have.' During high school my fear fantasy was getting pregnant. As a result I was a virgin until . . . incredible . . . here I was eighteen in the Haight-Ashbury, right? Had been going with this man, Gary, for years, but I always said, 'I will not be the shell-shocked victim that has to go home and confront the mother.' And naturally my fears were realized—I got pregnant.

"We had the big psychedelic wedding in San Francisco, in Golden Gate Park with the Hindu priest with the Roman Catholic crucifix around his neck, the flowers and the incense, and everybody's chanting *om*. The parents are there sitting on grass mats wearing sunglasses 'cause they'ɪe crying and devastated by the whole number because this can't be happening. They're Southern and upper crust and a bit snobby by tradition.

"We arrive back at the pad, which is a typical hippie crash pad, six or eight people who'd come for the wedding. All of a sudden I start bleeding profusely. I'm starting to miscarry, right? I'm bleeding like crazy. We were sharing our bedroom with this other woman—Jennifer. We get back and Gary gets in bed and Jennifer's there. So Gary rolls over and says to me, 'Do you mind'—while I'm bleeding, mind you—'if I have a nice little roll in the hay with sister Jennifer?' In the *same* single bed, right? I'm *crushed* up against the wall, right? I said, 'No, that's just *fine*, Gary! I just hope y'all won't mind if I have a cigarette.' I remember saying, 'I wish you'd be a little quieter.' He got mad at me for making such a request."

Lamar Jean and her husband then joined with several other couples to start a commune in Oregon. But it was impossible to sweep jealousy under the rug. For starters, there were no rugs:

"I'd have to say we were the classic children of the white middle class—educated, pretty well read, and totally confident we could thrive in the wilderness—even though the closest I'd been to roughing it was reading an L. L. Bean spring catalog. Well, once things got going we all spent six days a week going around being spiritual and enlightened and terribly loving, being terrific examples to others. Then on Sundays as a kind of spiritual exercise we'd all take acid. And *that's* when the defenses would break down and a lot of repressed emotions like jealousy would break out like brush fires. You just couldn't make it go away by pretending you had risen above it. Eventually we had to admit that we were just as vulnerable as any other normal human being to feelings of jealousy, resentment, and competitiveness.''

Contrary to their reputation for sexual openness, and to some of the examples cited here, most communes had surprisingly little in the way of group marriages, open relationships, or long-term sexual sharing. Certainly in rural communes, monogamous coupling was the rule rather than the exception.

Laurence Vesey, a professor of history at the University of California at Santa Cruz, wrote a very thorough study called *The Communal Experience*. When interviewed for this book, he reported that:

"Pair bonding at communes was quite prominent, despite its inconsistency with the communal tradition. For example, the classic approach to communes in the nineteenth century— say, the Oneida community or some of the turn-of-the-century anarchist groups—was to reduce or even eliminate pair bondings in order to let the energy flow through the group as a whole. What's so striking about so many [New Age] communes is the extent to which they reproduce a rather familiar conventional picture of two by two.

"People who grew tired of the commune or encountered problems with relationships there found it easy to merely drift on and go elsewhere.''

It seems that jealousy on communes was as prevalent and as challenging as in more conventional sectors of society. Professor Vesey believes that individualism had much to do with the failure of the communal movement, that allegiance to oneself was far stronger than the goal of communal society.

9   Limelighting
Jealousy

Lou Gottleib is one of the most colorful and energetic personalities I know. A tall, athletic, bearded man with imposing horn-rimmed glasses and a booming voice, Lou strides into a room and transfixes everyone present by narrating some recent comic adventure. Lou does it well, too—for he's a member of the Limelighters, one of the most successful and popular folk music trios. A smash hit in the 1950s, the group is resurrected each year and again plays to packed houses around the country. Only this time Lou's wearing sandals and flowing cotton gowns. Audiences love him. He personifies "irrepressible."

In 1966 Gottleib founded Morningstar Ranch, an hour's drive from San Francisco, and attempted to transfer the land deed to God. Figuring he was acting then as the Lord's agent, he invited *anyone* to live there.

When I first met Lou in 1968, several hundred people had taken up his offer. Lou, who incidentally has a Ph.D. in musicology, lived in a tiny chickencoop with room only for a piano, a bed, and a hot plate. He was buoyant and good-humored, not at all dismayed by extensive publicity, lawsuits from his neighbors and the county, or the twenty-four-hour circus surrounding him.

These days Lou is busy touring. The day of his interview he was puttering about his spacious San Francisco flat, alternately practicing classical piano ("for my concert debut at fifty") and entertaining several friends with one-liners. Here are some excerpts from his pronouncements on jealousy:

Lou's Views on the Beast

"The worst thing about jealousy as far as I'm concerned is that it seizes your consciousness. A thief in the night. You want to think about music, about money, and suddenly it has you. Involuntary. You can't control it. It's a terrible oppression because you're thinking about it when you don't want to be thinking about it.

"The best thing I've heard about jealousy in the longest time is a guy who owned two golden cocker spaniels. They were brother and sister with pedigrees from here to here. And he kept them to one litter a year so they would breed really first-class dogs. He kept her in an enclosure so that she wouldn't get the wrong stud. Everything was going great until about the fourth year when she came into estrum . . . and nothing happened. Her brother wouldn't mount her. So you know what the owner did? He got *another* male cocker spaniel and put *him* outside the wire enclosure. And the dog inside the enclosure fucked the female until he was *cross-eyed*! The owner's conclusion and mine is that jealousy plays a very big part in procreation. It guarantees *heat*. Jealousy will make you horny. There's no doubt about that. Like you've never been in your life. Definitely.

"Another thing about jealousy: the opposite of love is not hate but *indifference*. The real lover *wants* to be jealous. He wants that bite in the solar plexus. He wants that feeling. Without that it's, y'know, good friends, cosmic mates, this, that, and the other. Huggsies and so on. But it's not love, baby. . . .

"The thing that determines real love is the nose. *The nose knows!* Your real love smells exquisitely, gorgeously, enticingly, maddeningly attractive. And you're damn lucky if you run into it once. . . .

"A man likes that feeling of jealousy, that intensity. You really live intensely during the jealousy time. It's a kind of paranoia. The classic kind of paranoia—the coyote in the desert. It's something like that. Jealousy makes you aware—heightens your awareness of everything, particularly the activities of the beloved.

"The thing that is really crazy is that when you cause jealousy, you usually don't try. Setting out to make someone jealous is rarely successful. Jealousy, real jealousy, comes by random normal behavior. But for the lover it seems as though it's intentional, an attempt to destroy his or her equanimity. But it *does* make you horny. . . .

"I knew a cat in L.A. who was seven years with the wrong woman. I'd go see him and he'd say, 'Did you *see* her? Did she *call* you? *I'll kill the bitch!*' I've seen him with his muscles in spasms, he was so crazy. I would laugh at him and say, 'You don't know how ridiculous you look.' And he'd say, *'Ridiculous, huh, ridiculous!'* It went on for *seven* years. I asked him, 'What does she do for you?' And he said, 'She turns me *on!*' He was like a human fly. She lived up on the fifth floor and would lock all the doors and he would be climbing up on the outside of the building to get in. And they got married—they thought that would cure it. Ha-ha!

"There's no doubt that people in the throes of jealousy are oblivious of everything else, completely crazy in the sense that real psychos are. They're really strong and they can do anything."

Lou on Pregnant Jealousy

"I'll tell you when you learn jealousy. When women want to get pregnant, they're usually monogamous. And it is a very rare woman who can ball three guys and get pregnant and not know which one is the father. In general, most women want to know who the father of their child is.

"During the pregnancy you aren't going to go to the store alone, you aren't going to go anywhere alone, they are going to be with you. And then you start getting into that bag—together, together, together—you and your cosmic mate. And then comes the time when the child is already eight months old, he's off the tit, one thing and another. And her normal looking around begins.

"Or it may start with you. In the middle of the pregnancy you may say, 'Boy, that other chick really looks good,' and boing!—you've driven a nail into the fetus. You didn't think about it. And she's thinking, Here I am—blown in the body—he's thinking someone else looks good. Nobody looks at me that way now. In fact, that's the only thing my old lady didn't dig about pregnancy: 'Nobody hits on you when you're pregnant.'

"I'm a pregnant-lady freak myself. I think they're the most beautiful, but you can rarely ball a strange pregnant lady. They're not into that. And it is during that period that the nail is driven in and the attempt to extract it is extremely difficult. I think probably, if you want to play it safe and lead a dull life, the true monogamous relationship is the safest route. But who wants it? I'm very happy to have known jealousy and I look forward to it again, to tell you the truth. I want to see who the next one is that makes me jealous. It could be a man. That's the next thing it might be interesting to see. It might be a Gustave Aschenbach *Death in Venice*—type trip. What is there to fear?''

Lou's Cure for Jealousy

''I have found that the cure for jealousy comes from hatha yoga. Jealousy is an involuntary grab in the solar plexus, when you feel the beloved is having a better time than you are somewhere else. The thing you should do is immediately relax the muladhara chakra. That's the complex of sphincters that controls micturition, parturition, defecation, ejaculation, and every other bodily function that exerts expulsive energy. In Sanskrit they call it the apana. The muladhara chakra in Sanskrit anatomy is the root psychic center, located one inch above the perineum.

''In other words, if you talk about the forearm, it is manipulated by the triceps and the biceps. If you press down, the biceps is relaxed and the triceps is contracted. If you push up, the biceps is contracted and the triceps is relaxed. Sphincters are different from any other kind of muscle. Like your asshole. With your asshole, you can only clench and relax. That's the way the great piano players control rhythm. They clench their ass on the back beat: ONE—clench! TWO—clench! THREE—clench! FOUR—clench! And if you want to, retard your clench longer. So when that [jealousy] bite comes, you relax the anal sphincter. You transform the energy from this chakra, which is the solar plexus, into ecstasy.

''You can relax it anyplace. You can walk along and relax the anal area. In the whispered teachings of hatha yoga, the way they teach you to control micturition—peeing—is to piss half a stream. In other words, you're pissing, then cut your amp down to about one-half. That way you gain control over that particular sector—the contraction of that root center is called the mula bandha. I think the best cure for jealousy physiologically is relaxing that complex of sphincters.

"It works magically. It even works automatically, so that jealousy can be transformed into bliss immediately and if possible involuntarily and automatically. Let go—uncut your ass—and immediately a blissful sensation happens.

"As for my current goddess, I'm never jealous. Not of her. She's beautiful in every respect."

At this point one of Lou's listeners spoke up: "But, Lou, remember that day when her friend arrived and you told me you walked in and made a very uncomfortable scene?"

Lou (turning with a surprised look): *I?!?*
Listener: Yeah, you told me it was very uncomfortable.
Lou (quickly turning back, speaking with gusto): Please believe me, he's crazy, he's dreaming! These guys . . . please *believe* me, I have felt jealousy, real jealousy. Only it's all behind me now, that's all.

I once met Chief Alex Joseph, the best-known American polygamist. In 1976, Joseph had nine wives and wanted more.

Polygamy was part of the Mormon religion until the 1890s, when church elders announced God had directed that the practice be abandoned. God changed His mind about polygamy a year after the United States Congress banned the practice. But an estimated 25,000 to 35,000 Americans still live in polygamy, particularly in the Western states of Arizona, Idaho, and Nevada, and in Utah, where Alex Joseph and his family reside.

Joseph gets around the polygamy laws simply by skipping legal marriage ceremonies. He says the biggest problem in one-to-one relationships is jealousy, but he doesn't think it's a problem for him. He told a newspaper reporter:*

My wives can't get jealous of me; what's there to be jealous about? There isn't any possibility in the world of me stepping out on my wife. Your woman is afraid you're going to find somebody you prefer to her, and that is a threat to your relationship. But my wives only hope that I'll bring somebody home who can be added to our relationship.

How many truly monogamous men are there really? How many men are there who in their entire lifetime confine their sexual activity to one mate? Not many, if any. Why not acknowledge that and begin to live with it? The only difference between me and the average guy is that I do it out in the open.

Judy Joseph said her husband sleeps with his wives one at a time. Sexual jealousy crops up but the wives try to deal with it.

It's all a matter of seeing reality and taking the unknown out of it. I know Alex loves Pamela, for instance, and Pamela loves Alex, and they have a sexual relationship. That doesn't scare me. I love Alex and he loves me and we have a sexual relationship. Why should it be some fearsome thing to me that he is staying with another girl?

*Michael Seiler, "Monogamy Is 'Unnatural,' Man with 9 Wives Says," *Los Angeles Times*, February 9, 1976.

Pamela Joseph thought sexual jealousy was constructive in their home.

> If I see somebody who's got something really going for her in her relationship with Alex, I say to myself that's something I'd really like to have, too, and I see something maybe I should work on more.

According to Joanie Joseph, what jealousy exists in their family is petty.

> Like I'll walk into the living room and somebody else comes in and kisses Alex, and I'll think, am I going to be unhappy about that? Getting into the habit of choosing to be happy about that kind of thing is a good habit to cultivate.

Life for Alex Joseph and his family may really be as idyllic as they claim, but I can't conclude that polygamy or any other external change in social structures is the answer to problems of jealousy. Changes in individual attitudes and behavior is the answer, at least for most of us.

In the book *Group Marriage,** Larry and Joan Constantine report on their study on "multilateral marriages." They found that four-fifths of the groups they studied had problems with jealousy. The respondents ranked jealousy third among all problems of group marriage. The book contains fascinating information, like this observation about marriage involving two couples: "Without any intention, some sense of competition and comparison often arises from this configuration."

The book, which I found to be the best single source of information on jealousy, even though it focuses on the group experience, contains helpful specific hints for families

---

*New York: Macmillan, 1973.

like that of Chief Alex Joseph: "Fixed rotation is an equalizer and leaves no one out, minimizing the potential for jealousy, or so its proponents argue."

A general application of this recommendation, helpful to people in any sort of relationship, would be: make sure no one is left out.

10 Coping with Coupling

Women have always been called the "jealous sex," but in all my explorations on the subject one truth begins to stand out. Men are even more vulnerable to sexual jealousy than women. At first I thought this was a false perception, based on my own inordinate jealousy, that only by comparison to me did the women I know seem less prone to jealousy. Then I wondered whether I was choosing women unusually tolerant to what in retrospect I realized was blatant male chauvinist behavior. Or could it have been the general (if grudging) acceptance by women of a sexual double standard?

But all the information I gathered through interviews and other research led to the same curious conclusion. Women possess an apparently superior ability to ward off certain jealous feelings. Obviously women do get very jealous, but they usually require more provocation than men.

What is the reason? The answer was provided by the

work of Dorothy Dinnerstein, a feminist author and professor at Rutgers University. Professor Dinnerstein has developed a theory connecting sexism in Western society to the dominant role women traditionally play in child-rearing practices. Only when men share this responsibility, she believes, will we be able to solve the problems that threaten not only our personal relations but the future of life on this planet. Her theory explains the basis for our sexual double standard and why women may be less sexually possessive and jealous than men.

In her book *The Mermaid and the Minotaur: Sexual Arrangements and Human Malaise,** Dinnerstein details the way "female dominated child care guarantees male insistence upon, and female compliance with, a double standard of sexual behavior." The chapter most directly pertinent to jealousy is called "Higamous-Hogamous," after the Dorothy Parker rhyme:

> *Higamous hogamous, woman's monogamous.*
> *Hogamous higamous, man is polygamous.*

Dinnerstein states flatly that men are sexually more possessive than women, that women are less free than men to seek "selfish sexual pleasures," and that women more than men associate sex with emotional involvements.

According to Dinnerstein the male's tendency toward a sexual double standard and the female's tendency to consent to this double standard both originate in infancy, in the differing relationships of boys and girls to their mothers. We have already seen how jealousy first arises when a baby senses its mother's attention directed elsewhere. Other people who claim the mother's attention and, especially, her body are, Dinnerstein says, "resented competitors for a vital resource."

*New York: Harper Colophon Books, 1977.

Professor Dinnerstein argues that when a man makes love to a woman, the source of the pleasure he feels comes from outside himself, from a female body, just as a female body gave him pleasure as an infant. If the inhabitant of that female body chooses to ''bestow its resources on a competitor,'' she provokes jealousy, she brings the male back to the painful situations in which mother did not exclusively belong to baby.

A woman is also vulnerable to distress when faced with sexual competition, but less so than a man for several reasons, Dinnerstein says. For a woman, the situation is more complex since she has, in a real sense, become the archetypal mother figure herself. Her body has the same configuration as the one that originally nurtured her. Because a man's body size, genitals, voice quality, skin texture, and gestures usually differ so from a woman's, a male's sexual infidelity cannot conjure up so vividly for a woman that original and profound infantile sense of loss. What's more, the woman-raised woman inevitably feels a greater sense than a man that she carries within herself the power of the original dominant parent. She is more self-sufficient because a rival cannot take away what is within her, i.e., her essential womanhood.

On the other hand, Dinnerstein continues, the woman-raised man feels that the original source of life and comfort will always be found outside himself. In order to have a sense of reliable access to this source, he wants a woman to give her sexual attention to him exclusively.

Jealousy is more complex in women for another reason, Dinnerstein states. The girl's original love, like the boy's, is a woman—her mother. A child of either sex has earlier and therefore more powerful ties to its mother than to its father. Male children usually form a basic primitive attraction toward females. Female children also have this basic primitive attraction toward females. As a result, the adult woman's jealousy is more complicated. When she imagines sex between her man and a female rival, the thought of intimate contact with the woman isn't so disturbing to her as thoughts of same-sex contact might be for a man. After all, her earliest sensual pleasures came from the body of another female.

Professor Dinnerstein feels that even if a man might be sexually excited by thoughts of his lover having sex with another male, these thoughts are likely to be suppressed as shameful. Whereas for a woman thoughts of physical contact with another woman seem more acceptable because another woman, after all, provided her first physical comfort. Suppressed erotic feelings toward a rival can create the most violent types of jealous rage due to guilt and shame.

A fact related to the double standard is that sexual excitement is more strongly fixed to personal feelings in women than in men, she says. Women are less afraid of being plunged back into helpless infancy by falling in love because they have become mother figures themselves. Women do not so easily separate physical love from emotional love the way many men do (as a defense against dependency, hence vulnerability) for these reasons:

1. Women's continuing economic and social inferiority makes them emotionally dependent on men.
2. Sex is more serious for women because they can become pregnant.
3. The woman may more easily give herself over to sensuality when combined with emotional involvement because romantic love evokes the original primitive infantile love ties. She doesn't fear complete involvement as a man might, because she doesn't dread a possible loss as a man might. She cannot lose as much of her original love, for it now is partly within herself.

4. Women more easily melt into the personality of the person who gives them physical pleasure because, when they were infants, the physical identification and response was easier with a same-sex parent. A girl infant's identification with her mother is fairly effortless; a boy's is somewhat more difficult, and later he holds back more.

Dorothy Dinnerstein concludes: "As long as it is women who are mainly in charge of children the double standard will survive."

Her ideas about causes for the sexual double standard are controversial, but she seems to present the best explanation for the observable fact that women can tolerate far more than men before displaying jealousy. This is not to say that women don't get very jealous. Of course they do. But they are less vulnerable to the emotion than men.

Child-rearing practices may or may not change substantially, but we can do our best meanwhile not to encourage a double standard in our own conduct.

Among the most important agreements we can make are promises to ourselves. "Do unto others as you would have others do unto you" seems a reasonable way to act at any time. By including the Golden Rule in one's code of sexual ethics, a person prone to jealousy can greatly reduce irrational fears.

Many friends contributed advice, information, and anecdotes for this book. One evening a young, single neighbor named Victor dropped by and described "a situation that hasn't made anybody jealous just yet."

For several months he had carried on a mild flirtation with Natalie, the attractive wife of a boutique owner. He had fantasized about sleeping with her but hadn't thought seriously of pursuing the matter since she was married and had given him no real encouragement. But then things changed over a period of weeks. Natalie confided that her marriage was less than ideal, that she was bored. She even hinted she'd already had one casual liaison. The signals were clear.

Victor continued. "Yesterday we had lunch and Natalie announced that her husband was leaving tomorrow for a week in Hawaii and she'd like to see me." I asked what his feelings were.

"I'm of two minds about it. On the one hand, Natalie really turns me on and I'd love to jump into bed with her. Sleeping with her would be a lot of fun. On the other hand, I feel uncomfortable because she has a husband and I'd be back-dooring him. If my wife were getting it on with some other guy while I was away, I'd really be upset."

"Do you know how Natalie's husband would react?" I asked.

"No, I've only met him once," Victor answered.

"Are you afraid he might find out?"

Victor thought for a moment. "No, it's not that really. I guess I just feel uncomfortable about messing with a marriage. It would be different if I were falling in love with Natalie and ready to get involved. . . . But, on the other hand, maybe one night wouldn't do any harm."

I asked Victor to let me know what he'd finally decided. A week later he phoned and reported he'd declined Natalie's invitation. "I don't look at it as any great moral triumph," he added. "I was really looking out for number one. I guess in the long run I didn't want to find myself someday in her husband's shoes."

Victor could also have argued: "After all, I'm not trying to steal Natalie or destroy her relationship. It's Natalie who wants an outside involvement, and I should let her decide whether or not her marriage can take the strain."

I believe the choice is best made by examining your own feelings and intentions measured against the hoary old Golden Rule.

This is not to suggest that the only right move was declining Natalie's invitation. In fact, if you were in Victor's place, you might have bedded down with her without qualms. I'm only suggesting a way of thinking about such a situation. Ask yourself, "Would I care if my wife (or husband or lover) were to sleep with another while I'm away?" If the answer is yes, there's a strong likelihood sleeping with Natalie would contribute to your own vulnerability to jealousy. Note that the point of reference here is *you*.

The advantage to the Golden Rule approach is that you can act with a clear conscience *regardless of the option you choose*. In the future you'll have more confidence that others will respect your feelings in the same way. And as you trust others more, you will likely feel more secure in your relationships and thus less vulnerable to jealousy, *no matter what actually happens*.

As part of their study of group relationships, the Constantines, authors of the book *Group Marriage*, observed various coping mechanisms involved in jealousy. They noted four types of behavior: (1) antagonistic behavior, (2) isolational behavior, (3) redefinitional behavior, and (4) problem-solving behavior.

Antagonistic behavior involves fighting, quarreling, shouting, and other signs of anger, rage, and revenge. These acts are directed toward the lover or rival, but more often toward the lover.

Antagonistic behavior has some value, unless it is prolonged, since it keeps the parties in contact.

Isolational behavior involves withdrawal and separation from the lover. The withdrawal may be complete or partial.

A jealous person may withhold things the lover values, such as sex.

Isolational behavior hampers resolution of the problem, especially if it's habitual. Fighting at least involves some communication.

Redefinitional behavior involves intellectualizing and rationalizing, or attempting to redefine the problem. People using this method of coping with jealous feelings externalize the problem or use mechanisms of displacement. Instead of focusing anger on or withdrawing from a lover, they focus on a concept. For example, extramarital sex might become the common enemy.

Redefinitional behavior doesn't actively prevent reintegration of the couple, but neither is it very useful.

Problem-solving behavior, the most mature and constructive means of coping with jealousy, includes rational discussion of the meaning and possible resolution of the problem. This behavior is integrative and highly functional. The Constantines suggest the jealous person be aided in identifying his or her real feelings by asking what the feelings are and encouraging their expression.

People can learn to outgrow all types of jealousy except that related to the loss of satisfaction of true needs, which vary from person to person and can range from companionship to sex. If a loved one devotes less time to a need and no other relationship fills this need, we experience functional jealousy. People don't seem to outgrow jealousy arising from a complete or partial loss of need satisfaction, nor does it seem in their best interests to do so.

The Constantines identify these factors tending to enhance security and thus reduce the possibility of jealousy:

1. *A strong commitment or covenant between individuals.* The more intense the commitment, and the more it's expressed in terms of permanence,

the lower the threat of loss. If the loved one is perceived as committed on the basis of emotional investment, this enhances feelings of security more than an "as long as things are groovy" attitude does. Intermediate in effect is a commitment based on ideology, like "Marriage is forever."

2. *The length of the relationship.* The longer a relationship lasts, the more secure its participants feel.

3. *Individuation.* If each party to a relationship is regarded as unique (hence irreplaceable), this leads to feelings of security.

4. *Alternate sources of satisfaction.* Alternate sources of things valued in the relationship with a loved one increase a sense of security. The threat of losing the loved one thus does not mean losing all things one values. This, paradoxically, is compatible with the preceding idea of individuation, since an individual may be unique *in toto*, yet be the source of many separate things, each of which is obtainable elsewhere.

5. *Age.* Jealousy does generally decline with age. As we mature we generally learn better how to differentiate functional from dysfunctional jealousy. Functional jealousy is a response to a real threat. Dysfunctional jealousy is a response to an imagined threat.

A recurring theme found in the many self-help books on the market today is the importance of independence and self-assurance. Each authority puts it a different way. In *The Do-It-Yourself Psychotherapy Book,** Dr. Martin Shepard, a psychiatrist, points out that jealousy usually

*New York: Dutton, 1976.

involves blaming someone—either yourself or some other person—for the events leading to the jealous feelings. He says, "No one can ever hope to find self-contentment until that person is content to be truly and simply him or herself." Blaming is useless and frustrating. Blaming yourself or others not only causes conflict but also restricts your growth, adds to guilt feelings, and perpetuates the feeling that others control your life.

Psychologist Wayne Dyer, author of *Your Erroneous Zones* and *Pulling Your Own Strings,* confirms the idea that jealousy involves a loss of control of one's own life. He describes jealousy as "a form of slavery in which you are the slave and someone else is your emotional master."

Couples who support each other's freedom and autonomy are building security and reducing vulnerability to jealousy.

If your partner or lover has activities that don't include you, you have the option to consider that time as time given to you, not taken away from you. The richer your life, the less you'll be fearful and suspicious of what a loved one is doing.

Dr. Philip Zimbardo, a Stanford University psychologist, stresses the importance of balancing dependence with autonomy. He reiterates that lovers and mates are not possessions to be tucked away until needed, and that freedom is necessary for the growth of both partners. To maintain self-respect and interest, each partner must have a separate identity. In his book *Shyness: What It Is, What to Do About it,** Dr. Zimbardo advises:

1. Choose friends and situations that make you both comfortable. Otherwise, enjoy them separately.
2. Don't expect a partner to meet the expectations of others.

*Menlo Park, Calif.: Addison-Wesley Publishing Co., 1977.

3. Partners should support each other's interests in independent activities and friendships. One resulting benefit will be more new things to share with each other.
4. Work together at solving problems. Fight openly and fairly.
5. Don't sulk or clam up when problems arise. Anxiety or anger isn't relieved by silence.
6. Encourage a sense of humor. Laughter alleviates the distress of human mistakes and foibles.

Helping a Jealous Partner

Coping with a jealous partner may be just as difficult as coping with our own jealous feelings. But recognizing and preventing jealousy greatly benefits both parties. Drs. Lynn Smith and Gordon Clanton* advise that couples frequently reaffirm the special nature of their relationship, assure each other that whatever else happens, their relationship is primary. Couples who participated in their research on jealousy made some suggestions:

1. Consider sharing all details with a partner. Some people want to know everything and their suspicions will thus be reduced. Others don't really want to hear the specifics. Decide between you how you wish to handle this information.
2. If you suspect some activity might upset your partner, discuss it first, not afterward.
3. Partners can do what they like as long as they keep it to themselves and don't reveal their activities to neighbors and children.

*Fredelle Maynard, "The Green-Eyed Monster," *Woman's Day*, June 14, 1978, p 164.

4. Partners should make an agreement between themselves whether or not outside sex is all right, as long as it doesn't involve emotional commitments.
5. Outside relationships may be agreed to as long as the other person is unknown and won't be encountered.
6. You may decide that each partner may have one night a week free. Remember, the fuller your life, the less you'll imagine or resent the possible wandering of a partner.

Dealing with jealous feelings in yourself or someone else is easier if you can separate and define the components that cause anxiety. First, admit to the feelings of jealousy. Recognize that jealousy can be too diffuse and overpowering to cope with unless its causes, immediate and chronic, are understood. Look at your feelings to see exactly what you are experiencing. Here are some steps to follow suggested by Dr. Robert Blood*:

1. Are you afraid you'll lose your partner completely?
2. Do you feel deprived of your partner's company, without fearing complete loss?
3. Are you envious of the pleasure you imagine your partner is having?
4. Do you feel betrayed?
5. How do you feel toward the rival?
6. Do you have a sense of personal failure?

San Francisco psychiatrist Stephen Levine also believes in the value of breaking jealousy down to its components: "What I do in therapy is teach the person how to think about it. For example, when you get jealous, the first thing

---

*Dr. Robert Blood, quoted in "The Green-Eyed Monster" by Fredelle Maynard, *Woman's Day*, June 14, 1978.

to do is write down what happened. The objective reality. And pay attention to details, really attend to that. Re-create the situation, even down to what music, if any, was playing. Then, what thoughts did you have about it? Perception is more than a process of seeing. It's attaching meaning to what is seen.

"The patient often assumes that 'that thing out there hurt me,' when in fact that person may be causing the jealousy within him or herself. A lot of times what the patient is experiencing is a conditioned response learned in infancy, a way of responding that may have worked effectively then, but which is totally out of place in an adult. And by closely reexamining responses, the patient may also reexamine values, religious upbringing, his or her entire background.

"By taking a close look at the causes of these emotions, it's often possible to change our responses. A patient may feel he or she 'should' feel this way, or 'should' do that. The therapist must exorcise a lot of 'shoulds.' "

Eric Berne, M.D., was the founder of Transactional Analysis, which he defined as "a theory of personality and social action, and a clinical method of psychotherapy based on the analysis of all possible transactions between two or more people." If you and your emotions are controlled by others, he said, you can never really be happy. That's why he stressed the importance of autonomy.

Berne taught that mature relationships involve a balance between dependence and independence. In his book *Games People Play*, he wrote:

   The attainment of autonomy is manifested by the release or recovery of three capacities: awareness, spontaneity, and intimacy.
   Awareness means the capacity to see [things] in

one's own way, and not the way one was taught. . . .
Awareness requires living in the here and now, and
not in the elsewhere, the past, or the future.

Spontaneity means options, the freedom to choose
and express one's feelings from the assortment
available. It means liberation . . . from the compulsion
to play games and have only the feelings one was
taught to have.

Intimacy means the spontaneous, game-free candid-
ness of an aware person. . . .

I met Dr. Berne once, and shortly before his death we
had a long telephone conversation while he was writing a
review of my first book. But I've known his closest
professional associate, Claude Steiner, since we were both
college students. I remember advising Claude during that
time about a matter of love. I guess he sought my counsel
because at nineteen I was a year older than he. Now he's
in a position to advise me—and you.

Claude Steiner, Ph.D., is a psychologist, best-selling
author, and cofounder of the Radical Therapy Institute in
Berkeley. His perspective on marriages, relationships, and
the role of jealousy is intriguing. In an interview for this
book, he described two kinds of jealousy; one related to
power, the other to love.

Power jealousy, he feels, has nothing to do with love or
affection but rather with threats to self-esteem related to
concepts of territory, property, and social status:

"People have a tendency to relate to certain parts of
their environment as their territory, their property, their
domain. This happens more with men, but it happens with
women too. A certain person tends to become one's domain.
Whether or not you love that person has nothing to do with
it. Your territory has been invaded by some other person,
so you feel jealousy.

"You'll find a man who looks at a strange woman and likes her. Another man next to the woman looks at her, and the first man is immediately jealous because he is already putting some sense of territory on her and has a competitive reaction, even though he doesn't even know her. That's kind of the extreme.

"Or you have a woman who is relating to another woman, but doesn't really love her, is just relating to her. The moment that second woman approaches another person the feelings of jealousy go up. These feelings, which appear connected with love, really have to do with competitiveness and territory. That type of jealousy is destructive, the type that people really want to get over. They sense that it's no good."

As for jealousy between lovers, he sees it as not only normal and expected but useful. For example, if a man and woman have formed a loving relationship lasting several years that is characterized in part by their being faithful to each other, a new love interest for either partner will cause the other partner to feel that something has changed. Trust has been violated, an agreement (whether or not articulated) has been breached, and the result is normal jealousy.

Steiner believes that few relationships (including marriage) involve either party spelling out ground rules regarding matters like outside sexual interests. Nonetheless, there exist well-understood unspoken agreements.

"Let's say you are in a relationship with someone and have a certain understanding of what you will give each other. If that understanding, that agreement, is broken in some way, then you're going to feel the jealousy that comes from loss of something you want from that person.

"For instance, if I'm in a relationship with a woman and I want to have sex more than she wants to, I may not have any problem with that, I just realize what her needs are. But if I then find out she is having sex more often with someone else, I immediately feel jealous, not because she is with someone else, but because she is giving someone something I want for myself, part of an agreement between us. I love that person, I want something from her, and I'm not getting it.

"I don't feel that type of jealousy is destructive or should be eliminated, because it comes from unfair arrangements between people. That type of jealousy is very reasonable. It is an index that something is wrong in the relationship and that something needs to be done. Any person who feels jealous in that way, I will support—to feel the jealousy and do something about it, to clarify the agreement, to go after the thing that is scarce. Jealousy in this instance is due to a scarcity of something. I think it's very valid, and I think it's foolish to try to hide it, to not feel it, because if you do you're going to get ripped off."

Steiner differentiates love jealousy from purely sexual jealousy. "It's the power thing mostly, with sexual jealousy. It's clear-cut territory. A woman's cunt is territory. Men have dealt with it as territory; they invade it, they rape it, they own it, they want to own it exclusively. It's the quintessence of territorial jealousy."

Steiner discussed the ways people attempt to reduce jealousy through unconventional relationships.

"Some people just cannot be monogamous. It doesn't work for them. They should avoid attempting relationships with people who need to be monogamous. The complications of monogamy can be dealt with as they come up if people decide to be monogamous. That can be done.

"There are several levels of monogamy. There is sexual monogamy and emotional monogamy. You can be one and not the other. You have to look below the surface. You can see two people in a nuclear family situation, but if you look closely at the behavior, the woman has a close woman friend that she goes away with on the weekends, no sex.

The man has a man friend that he goes away with some weekends, no sex. They have friends come in. They are loose about it when they go out with another person. Or they love another person. That still looks like a monogamous couple, but emotionally it isn't.

"You can have people who live in a commune and they're going crazy with jealousy all the time, never out of each other's laps, talk real hip, talk about not being jealous, and before you know it their behavior is totally nuclear-family, they're going to have a baby, or they're going to break up.

"Couple-ism is the oppression of single people by couples. The most blatant example is the groovy married couple who are bored and decide to open up their relationship. In order to do that they get in touch with a third person, and that's likely to be extremely oppressive to the third person. Everything that happens to the third person is going to be in the hands of the couple. The third one is usually a woman and she is sure to get ripped off. She's at their mercy and has no support or equality. They think it's great. She thinks she has the better of the deal, because of the old assumption that if you cut into someone else's territory you're getting away with something. But you're really getting ripped off. When people join together as a couple, they have much more power, that's the reason single people stay away from them—they have this aura, a thick mass you can't get through. Haven't you noticed that?

"As hard as it is to have a couple that works, three people is even harder. You have to check into things after six months or a year—a honeymoon is very common in all relationships. In that early part it's very high and they go out and talk about it and write books—a year later it's all over, finished. By the time the baby is born, it's all wrong.

"Let me tell you how we deal with jealousy in the Radical Therapy Institute. We feel that the scarcest things in our lives are good loving relationships. Everything else is completely available, practically, but love is just not coming across. It's just not happening too well, so we're very much into helping people develop good relationships. It's what we feel people need and are willing to help them get.

"Rules of relationships used to keep people on a course that often worked. Since the old rules are not being followed anymore, people are really confused.

"We have some rules of cooperation. We feel that only a cooperative relationship can really succeed. First of all, it is understood that there be no lies or secrets, because lies and secrets are the foundation for paranoia and jealousy. Most people assume that the best way to relate to people is not to tell them what's going on. It's very hard for people to recognize that truthfulness is an important part of a relationship.

"In order for jealousy not to develop you need absolute truthfulness. After all, there's no way to kid a lover about what's going on. There's only a way to confuse him about what's going on. Anyone who is walking around with a split brain, one half saying, 'My old lady is fucking someone,' and the other half saying, 'No, nothing is going on'—that alone is so confusing that's it's debilitating. One's mind gets completely boggled, whereas it's much easier to handle knowing if she wants to ball someone, or she's actually doing it, especially if you have worked up something cooperative.

"It's very difficult to do this in the middle of a relationship. You can't take a two-year relationship that's falling apart and say, 'Okay, everyone is going to be truthful.' That's not what I'm talking about. I'm talking about people entering a relationship agreeing that they will be completely truthful—and that is excruciatingly painful, but very important training for a whole lot of other things. To be truthful and know when you're telling the truth, because truthfulness implies not just that you're not lying, but that you're being expressive of what you're feeling. It's an education to be truthful.

"The other thing is that there be no behavior that we call power-play behavior—behavior which is designed to get something from somebody else against their will, not with their cooperation, competitive behavior. There's all sorts of behavior of that sort, but let's say, for instance, two lovers have a relationship going and one of them gets interested in someone else. His or her lover, instead of saying, 'I'm jealous, I don't want you to do this,' says, 'If you're getting it on with someone, I will too.' This is a maneuver to get something from someone against their will. It is not a cooperative decision.

"In a cooperative relationship the same thing would be handled by saying, 'I'm jealous, I don't want you to do this. If you're going to do this, I want the freedom to do something else. I feel like running out to make you jealous, but let's talk about it and see what we come up with.' Maybe the agreement will be that the person will say, 'It's not that important now if it's going to hurt you so much, but I do want to do this eventually. So I want to work toward an arrangement where I can have another lover once in a while, and it's okay if you have another lover' —and it gets talked out. There's a possibility that the person really wants to go out now and says, 'It's very important and I can't compromise on this. I'm sorry. What can I do to make it easier for you?' The other person might say then, 'Take a bath before you come to see me,' or 'Don't stay out after midnight.'

"So the first two rules to this business of cooperation are no secrets and no power plays. The third is no rescues.

What we call 'rescue' is when you do something you don't want to do, do more than half the work in any situation. In a cooperative relationship you do not do things you do not want to do, you do not allow yourself to put up with situations you do not want to be in. For you to go ahead and do something when you don't want to is a 'rescue.'

"Sure, you're going to go through changes no matter what you're into—polygamy, monogamy, married, unmarried, living together. The changes are there—unless you're the kind of person who goes in and out of relationships. There are people like that who relate until the hassles start and then go on to someone else. But after a while they'll be suffering because their life will be empty as hell."

11 Preventive Care

Jealousy feeds on itself. The more jealous we are, the more insecure we feel. The more insecure we feel, the more liable we are to experience jealousy. The opposite is also true: the more secure we feel, the less vulnerable we are to jealousy.

Jealousy is essentially a protective reaction based on survival instincts. A solid sense of self-esteem allows us to distinguish between true and false threats of loss.

We have seen how jealousy can seize and distort the rational mind. Jealousy *feels* the same whether justified or illogical. Its primitive force is one reason why efforts to confront it head-on are usually futile. Think of mastering jealousy as if it were a goal visible atop a sheer mountain face, unattainable by any direct route, even with ropes and pitons. We shall reach that goal indirectly but surely.

The information in this chapter was culled from many sources and represents the best available on what constitutes security and the means of maintaining or bolstering feelings of self-esteem. Let us begin by delineating some components of security.

Some Components of Security

1. *Secure people envision the world as a pleasant, friendly place.* How do you view the world you inhabit? Does it seem congenial, or hostile and threatening?

   The way you view your world is entirely your choice. Since you have the choice you might as well consider your world a source of endless opportunity for information, stimulation, pleasure, and well-being.

2. *Secure people regard others as essentially benevolent.* How do you view the other people who inhabit your world? You probably understand very well by now that their interactions with you depend on how you respond to them. Don't forget how much the quality of your encounters reflects what you emanate from within yourself. The people you meet will mirror your attitudes. You've heard these things before and you know they are valid. But it's easy to forget. So don't forget.

3. *Secure people tend toward optimism.* How will things turn out for you? In relationships? Your work? Family? Children? If you assume things will go well, you will have a better chance of succeeding.

   You needn't be a Pollyanna. You can keep in touch with reality while maintaining a positive attitude. Again, you have a clear choice of how you view things—positively or negatively. And positive thinking does have power.

4. *Secure people tend to be relaxed and stable.* Your home, family, relationships, work, and health should each contain elements producing in you a sense of ease, calmness, satisfaction, and security. If they do not, you can examine them and choose to improve upon them. Many methods are available for encouraging a calm, relaxed state. Seek out a means appropriate for you.

5. *Secure people are self-accepting.* You are fine just as you are. This does not contradict our plan to maintain and build further inner strengths, but you already possess admirable and powerful human qualities if you've been around long enough to read these words. Let those qualities shine through. When you have moments of self-doubt say to yourself, "I am fine just as I am. I am fine just as I am." It's true.

6. *Secure people tend to be outgoing and take an interest in others.* Don't forget the smiles, hellos, and other simple ways we can give psychological strokes to those we encounter. You enrich your life immeasurably when you become involved in the lives of others—friends, family, and even strangers. Try finding a social cause you can support and become involved. You needn't be extroverted to develop a sense of community. Keep in mind the photographs of earth you've seen taken from outer space.

7. *Secure people feel loved.* They have a sense of belonging, of togetherness, and believe others regard them with warmth. You feel stronger when you are surrounded by people you care for, and who care for you in return. But beware of belonging for the sake of belonging—of groups led by charismatic con artists.

8. *Secure people tend to be happy*. The route to happiness is indirect. Happiness is a side effect of aspects in life that are satisfying. While you can't directly attain happiness, you can reflect on activities in your life that have produced happiness in the past, and use them as a guide for your future conduct.

9. *Secure people tend to feel unconflicted*. Are your goals clear? Do you have goals? You will probably never be completely free of conflict in your life, nor is life without conflict ideal. But reducing conflicts in your goals and relationships will enhance feelings of security.

10. *Secure people possess realistic coping systems*. You can be optimistic, treat people kindly, be loving and loved, relaxed, outgoing, and happy, and still live in the real world.

Few people feel totally secure all the time, nor is it necessarily in their best interests to feel totally secure. Having a total sense of security is like being a rock, impervious to most assault, but unmoving and unfeeling.

Once you know and understand what's necessary to a good sense of self-esteem, you can act to strengthen these components within yourself.

The External You

Your internal states of mind and body can be assessed by observing the external you. Both the external and internal affect and reflect each other.

1. *Appearance*. You probably look at yourself in a mirror every day, but now put aside a full five or ten minutes and place yourself in front of a full-length mirror. Try it first with the clothes you

might usually wear, then without any clothes at all. Write down five physical aspects that please you, or that bring compliments from others. Now list five things that displease you.

You can't make yourself shorter or taller. But you can change many things about yourself if you so choose. You can lose weight or gain muscle. You can alter your posture. You can change your hairstyle. Even though you're probably fine just as you are, it's worthwhile to experiment with changes now and then.

List all the changes you could make if you so desired. Now check off the changes you will actually choose to bring about and list them separately. How will you begin to make these changes? Beside each item on your small list outline a plan. Make out a realistic schedule with goals possible for you to reach. Put the list and the schedule where you'll see them each morning near the mirror. Achieve those goals and congratulate yourself as you do. You deserve it.

2. *Nutrition.* The human body can tolerate a surprising variety of diets, but the effect of nutritious, as opposed to poor, food on mind and body can also be a revelation.

Make a list of everything you remember eating during the past three days. Include between-meal snacks and drinks. Were you eating the quality and quantity of food you know is best for you? Are you feeding yourself things you know are unhealthy? If you are unsure of what constitutes a nutritious diet, consult a library, a local health-department nutritionist, your doctor, or a healthy-looking food-store owner.

Keep track of your nutritional intake for the

next week. Chances are, simply recording what you eat and drink will enable you to make any necessary changes.

3. *Exercise and relaxation*. Specific exercise fads come and go, but there's little doubt you'll be healthier, feel better, and look better if you regularly give your body some sort of exercise. No need to torture yourself. Do something you enjoy, like tennis, bicycling, hiking, even running. And this is an apt place to recommend that you experiment with changing the kind of cosmetics or soap you use.

Relaxation is one of the paradoxical benefits of exercise. Your goal here is to take your mind away from its usual ruminations. Don't think too much! At least not about the same old things. Get back into the habit of reading for escape as well as self-improvement. Explore some of the many meditation techniques.

Many people rely too much on alcohol or other drugs for relaxation. What about you?

Make a list of the forms of exercise and relaxation you've had in the past week and the time spent on them. What changes can you make? Next week note any ways you've improved on your means of exercise and relaxation.

4. *Clothing*. Clothes are like a shell hanging on a shell. External on external. But they do reflect much about you. Perhaps it's time to get some different clothes. Most people feel better when they do. It's a simple way of making changes. Make sure the clothes you wear are really right for you. Think about comfort, color, and style, in that order. Ask some advice from a friend whose taste you respect. Take that friend shopping with you if possible.

You may be able to initiate all the preceding suggestions within a short period of time. Once you've begun, you're well on your way to building an armor of self-confidence against unreasonable jealousy or unreasonable reactions to jealousy. If you haven't already done so, get a notebook and keep track of the changes you've made and the suggestions and exercises that follow.

Value Your Time

When I first entered college my most valuable class was a one-unit course designed to teach first-year students good study habits. An early (1952) version of speed-reading was included, but most helpful was simply charting each day's activities, hour by hour. Tracking time in that fashion gives one a sense of which activities are valued and which should be valued.

A few years ago a younger friend said to me, "Chances are you've lived half your life already. How does that make you feel?" It made me feel like using my remaining time well. I wrote out those two sentences on a large piece of paper and tacked the paper to a wall of my office, where it is to this day. Try this yourself. Assume the average life-span is eighty years. Say to yourself, "Chances are you've lived [whatever fraction] of your life already. What will you do with the time remaining to you?"

To help you assess your priorities, make up a daily calendar sectioned by hours. Fill in this calendar accurately for at least two weeks (the longer the better). At the end of each week review and classify your activities. Are you using your time well? Do you want to emphasize some activities more than you have previously? Can you do so? How?

Make a check mark or asterisk by each activity that made you feel good. How did it take place? How could more of these activities take place?

Know Who You Are—Know What You Want

1. What are your values? List five principles by which you could guide your life. Make sure you follow them.

2. List ten good qualities about yourself. Memorize them and don't forget them.

3. Can you list ten things you don't like about yourself? Check off the qualities amenable to change and work on them. Forget the others.

4. List ten qualities you value in other people. Which do you possess? Could you make changes enabling you to obtain the others? Do you want to make these changes? Do you know how to make these changes?

5. List ten of the most important people in your life. Beneath each name, list five reasons why he or she is important to you.

6. List five long-range goals you hope to achieve someday.

7. List twelve projects or short-range goals you could achieve within the next year. Beneath each of those twelve projects, outline the steps by which they could be reached.

8. What are the ways in which the above twelve projects could help you achieve your long-range goals?

Become an Expert

When I was a third-year medical student, one of my instructors was a resident in internal medicine named Harvey. Harvey wanted to be an expert in some medical field, and chose the thyroid gland as his area of interest. Within a few months Harvey knew more about thyroid functions and dysfunctions than anyone else at our medical school.

Soon he was the standard consultant for any patient with a thyroid problem. I never forgot that lesson.

Choose some topic of interest to yourself and preferably to others as well. Read about it in a library, then take note of newspaper and magazine articles or television stories on the subject. You'll be surprised at how quickly you can learn most or all that is known about nearly any reasonably limited nontechnical area.

As you gain knowledge in your chosen field, try discussing what you've learned with friends and acquaintances. You'll also find it easier to initiate conversation with new people you encounter. Becoming an "expert" will make you more interesting to others and thus bolster feelings of self-esteem.

Once you've begun to build or strengthen generally your feelings of self-worth, you can work specifically on problems involving jealousy.

Changing the Script

1. Think about a recent episode in which a person or situation caused you unreasonable jealousy. Recall the time and setting. Pay attention to details like lighting and color. Remember everything that was said and done and what went wrong. This is scene one.

2. Now think of someone you like and respect, a self-confident person you believe has little trouble with jealousy. Put that person in the same situation you've just recalled. What could that person say or do differently to produce a better outcome? This is scene two.

3. Set up the original jealousy-provoking situation in your mind again. Go through the sequence of events as they occurred, but this time imagine the

more desirable words and actions coming from you. This is scene three.

Run through these three scenes over and over again, but each time make the third scene increasingly more vivid. Next time you start feeling jealous, consider changing the script.

Turn Down the Level

High anxiety levels often precede and predispose one to bouts of jealousy. One tense emotional state easily triggers another. When you know you're about to be in a stressful situation ripe for jealousy, take steps beforehand to relieve your anxiety.

1. Use your favorite means of relaxation. If exercise makes you tranquil afterward, then exercise. If you're a meditator, meditate. I know a psychiatrist who suggests this is a time for two stiff drinks. Medically, though, it's a dubious idea. A nice warm bath will not only relax you but make the following steps easier. If it's impractical to actually soak in the bathtub, put your feet in a pan of warm water. You may be surprised to learn how good it feels just to warm your feet this way. Next best is lying down and imagining you're in a warm tub or stretched out on a tropical beach. Think about a time and place when you felt happy, loved, and secure.

2. Now picture the situation about to take place. Based on what you know in advance, run the scene through your mind in detail. Imagine what might occur and the variety of your possible reactions. Concentrate on the response you find most desirable. Remember that you can change the script, so imagine a good outcome for the event about to take place.

3. Think of your past achievements, of compliments paid you by others. You may want to repeat some of them to yourself over and over. Many people take comfort from the previously mentioned simple mantra, "I am fine just as I am."

Desensitization

Desensitization is a technique often used to prevent certain annoying or debilitating allergies. The first step is to determine the allergen, or substance causing the allergy. Let's say it is found to be cat dander (shed skin cells). The allergy could be prevented by avoiding all contact with cats, but what if the patient is a veterinarian? The solution to this problem may be desensitization.

Desensitization begins by diluting a quantity of the allergen to such an extent that when injected beneath the skin it causes little or no reaction. The concentration of the injected substance is then increased slowly over a period of time. Gradually the body becomes desensitized to increasing doses of the allergen, until a point is reached when the patient has little or no reaction when exposed to the substance formerly causing the allergic reaction.

Desensitization can also be used for behavior modification. The "allergen" in this case is jealousy. Begin by remembering a time and place when you felt very happy and serene. Recall the scene in rich detail, create it in your mind. Is it warm or cold there? Is the air dry or humid? What are the landscape features? Can you remember characteristic scents? What are you wearing? If you prefer, make up such a scene from your imagination; choose your ideal spot. Now place your actual lover or love ideal in that wonderful scene at your side. Enjoy the place, the time, and your lover.

Next, with the same richness of detail, recall a situation

that caused you some jealousy—not a lot, but enough to produce mild discomfort. (You might choose a 2-point answer situation from Chapter 2, the Jealousy Diagnostic Index.) Spend a full 5 minutes running the distasteful episode through your mind. Now switch back to that first scene of happiness, serenity, and security and stay there for 5 minutes. Then back to the 2 + jealousy situation for 5 minutes, and finally return to your own vision of paradise for 5 minutes. Do this 20-minute desensitization exercise twice a day for seven days.

On the eighth day, increase the strength of the "allergen." Visualize a jealousy episode causing you more distress, a 3 + Jealousy Diagnostic Index answer, or its equivalent. Imagine that scene of distress for 5 minutes, then switch back to the scene of pleasure. Repeat as before, 20 minutes twice a day for seven days.

During the third week, use a 4 + situation from the Jealousy Diagnostic Index or its equivalent, switching from this most painful episode to the pleasurable scene, just as you've done during the previous two weeks.

If, at the end of three weeks, any of the jealousy scenes you've used causes pain, go back to a 2 + jealousy situation. Repeat the 20-minute, twice-daily exercise for two days, or until you feel no discomfort, whichever occurs first. Then advance to a 3 + situation with the same instructions, and finally to the 4 + situation.

If you still experience discomfort, drop this exercise for now, do others in this chapter, and resume the desensitization process in three weeks.

Role Playing

Changing your perspective can change your perceptions. Theater games can be useful psychological tools for these changes. Here's one among many.

You can do this exercise alone or with one or two other people. Let's assume you're alone. Pick a place where you won't be interrupted or overheard.

Arrange three chairs so that they face each other. Sit in one of them. Recall an incident that caused you jealousy. Imagine your lover or partner is in the second chair and the rival in the third chair. Start talking about the jealousy incident. Vent your rage or grief or shame. Tell them exactly how you feel and why. Yell at them. Tell them it's their fault, and why it's their fault.

Now switch chairs. Become your lover talking to you. Explain your view of the incident and how you feel about the jealousy it provoked.

Now go back to your own chair. Talk to the rival. Yell, threaten—however you feel. Then get in the rival's chair and become the rival talking to you and your partner.

If you want some privacy, remove one of the chairs. Just don't shoot yourself in a crime of passion!

12 Mastering Jealousy

As we have seen, jealousy is a complex emotion that can include feelings of anger, grief, fear, suspicion, and shame. These more basic components are part of our humanity, in fact part of mammalian nature, and have survival value. Since jealousy itself is observable in animals other than man, it is likely that this more complex emotion also originated as a protective instinct. Instincts die long and hard, even when they no longer have survival value, so it is not surprising that jealousy won't disappear simply because we wish it gone. But we can reduce it to an occasional annoyance and can certainly prevent it from being a destructive factor in our lives.

The combined reactions that characterize jealousy are first brought together in infancy. When an infant feels denied the nurture of its caring parent, senses the parent's attention directed elsewhere, it commonly responds by crying, yelling, screaming, or perhaps withdrawing. Later in life, circumstances involving a sense of loss may cause individuals to revert emotionally to an infantile stage, a time when the person who seemed lost provided not only love but life itself. The initial reaction will very likely to be the earliest response to jealousy—anger, rage, grief.

Jealousy in an adult commonly includes elements of shame—shame for still being subject to a painful emotion known since infancy. This feeling of shame is often mixed with rage when sexual jealousy includes not only loss of a loved one but contact with a rival via strong identification with the body of a loved one. It is also very likely that males and females in our culture vary in susceptibility to jealousy, depending on which parent was predominant in the earliest stages of child rearing.

Mature individuals can learn to outgrow certain types of jealousy—jealousy learned later in life, which is superimposed on reactions learned earlier, and thus more amenable to change. The types of jealousy people can eliminate most successfully have to do with status, control, possession, and exclusivity. The one type of jealousy that cannot, and probably should not, be eliminated involves a real threat of losing a loved one who satisfies truly felt needs.

Ample evidence exists in our own and other cultures that sexual sharing need not prompt jealousy. It is the meaning attached to the behavior in question that causes jealousy, not the behavior itself. Albert Ellis is another psychologist who points out that no one person can fulfill all the needs and desires of another. Yet from childhood we have been encouraged to believe that there exists one and only one ideal person meant for us. Once with that person we may find it difficult to comprehend emotionally how a partner may be sexually attracted to, much less love, another individual.

When romantic ideals of courtship and marriage clash so regularly with actual behavior, the predictable result is insecurity in relationships, which in turn fosters chronic jealousy. In *The American Sexual Tragedy,* Ellis writes that a belief in finding the "one and only" leads to a corresponding fear of losing this once-in-a-lifetime partner. What's more, idealizing one's partner inevitably sets up eventual disillusionment, which in turn breeds constant anxiety and insecurity, whether or not consciously experienced.

Among other factors that breed insecurity (and consequent vulnerability to jealousy), Ellis indicates the ego-involving character of choosing one's mate. Since partners are usually freely selected, the departure of one's partner from a relationship may mean a terrific loss of face. The fear of scandal, gossip (e.g., "He couldn't keep her, he didn't have what it takes"), and social ostracism feeds the anxiety.

Loss of face may also occur with covert sex outside a relationship. To find oneself the cuckolded man or the deceived woman can be a little like some victims of insensitive doctors and terminal disease—always the last to know, a predicament that suggests everyone else around you has known for some time. And even if gossip is not an element, the fact that a partner has slept with someone else may breed feelings of rejection or lowered sexual self-esteem. One feels a loser in a very competitive society where winning frequently is symbolized by sexually possessing another person.

The distressing rate of teenage pregnancies and a national divorce rate approaching 50 percent are sobering indicators of great changes occurring in our courtship and marriage customs. As these changes take place, we try to mesh our ingrained ideals with the facts of our lives.

Social contacts outside a relationship need not indicate loss of love, nor should they be necessarily viewed as rejection or betrayal. But we may feel insecure because our learned standards of behavior conflict with the current lack of social pressures, discouraging activities outside a formed relationship. Increased jealousy is one result of an inability to integrate learned behavior with these social realities.

So what to do about this shadow of love? Two things, at once simple and complex. The first is to understand the social, psychological, and personal manifestations of jealousy and to implement this knowledge. The second is realize to that the brighter we shine, the smaller the shadow cast by our love.

Most of us would prefer never to feel jealousy again and this is possible, though unlikely. But we know by now that there is both rational and irrational jealousy. And we know also that there are functional and dysfunctional means of coping with jealousy.

Preventing jealousy is far easier and more productive than dealing with the emotion once it appears, since we may then lose power over our rational thoughts and behavior. The process of reducing vulnerability to unjustifiable jealousy begins in infancy. By recognizing the origins of jealousy we can help raise children less inclined to experience the emotion. A good sense of self-esteem established in childhood can be maintained and bolstered by techniques outlined in Chapter 11, Preventive Care. These techniques include setting goals—realistic and specific goals—accomplishing them, and acknowledging to ourselves the work well done.

As adults we can reduce jealousy in those we care for. Don't be afraid to declare your feelings. Demonstrating the care you feel helps develop trust and security in relationships. Recognition and attention to a partner both in public and private will foster feelings of being special and worthwhile. Express your desires, doubts, and fears, and encourage your partner to do the same. Help create an atmosphere in which you and your partner share responsibility for giving each other reassurance and emotional support.

Remember that jealousy thrives on uncertainty and insecurity. We needn't make immutable rules, but we can certainly choose to let our feelings, wishes, and limits be clearly known.

Strong relationships maintain a fair mix of autonomy and dependence. One of the commonest defenses against jealousy is moving so far toward complete autonomy that no room remains for other people. Actually, this method is usually more a retreat from the dangers of emotional involvement, such as susceptibility to jealousy, than an active move toward autonomy. Barring emotional involvements to insure against jealousy also shuts out the possibility of true affection, and human beings can literally wither and die without affection.

Another common, and commonly flawed, means of preventing jealousy is through deceit—lies and omissions—the theory being, "What they don't know won't hurt them." This method is successful only when people agree to it beforehand, when they accept one another's need or desire for outside relationships, but can't accept knowing the details. Even so, deception often establishes an atmosphere of tension and insecurity, which easily breeds jealousy. Lies complicate thought processes and create detours in the mind that muddy direct and honest communication. A young woman I know once burned her feet by rubbing them against a wooden bench during a brief tryst in a sauna. "Where did those burns come from?" asked her roommate. "Oh, from my new boots," she quickly replied. Even little lies can accumulate to form a kind of psychic armor, impenetrable from without, but also impregnable to profound caring and love.

Whether or not couples choose to have outside relationships, they will best avoid jealousy by honest, clear discourse about feelings, desires, and needs, by offering mutual emotional support and reassurance, by maintaining separate as well as mutual identities and interests.

Jealousy is best regarded as a potentially valuable signal, analogous to a smoke detector, that will never be activated but which is nonetheless available and alert, guarding against true loss.

When I began this work, my intention was to find a total cure for jealousy, a means to eradicate this painful emotion altogether. I no longer believe it possible or even desirable to wholly eradicate jealousy, or at least the possibility of jealousy, at least for now. But it is possible and desirable to reduce or eliminate most instances of the jealousy we usually experience.

If jealousy ever loses its protective value, it will slowly die out, becoming less a part of our lives, like the vestigial fifth toe or the muscles that once enabled all humans to move the visible portion of the ear.

Changes in child-rearing practices and social structures may alter the causes of jealousy, but the potential for this emotion will never leave us entirely so long as we know love.

Appendix: Scoring and Interpreting the Jealousy Diagnostic Index

Once you've answered all the questions in the Jealousy Diagnostic Index (p. 12), tabulate your score according to the answers that follow.

Each answer has a value of from 1 to 4 points. The highest total number of points possible is 138, indicating someone with a great potential for jealousy. The lowest possible number of points is 50, indicating someone with a very high threshold for jealousy. Few if any individuals will score near these extremes.

PART 1

Question	True (points)	False (points)	Question	True (points)	False (points)
1.	1	2	7.	2	1
2.	3	1	8.	3	1
3.	3	1	9.	3	1
4.	3	1	10.	2	1
5.	3	1	11.	3	1
6.	2	1	12.	4	1

13.	1	2	**25.**	2	1
14.	3	1	**26.**	3	1
15.	3	1	**27.**	4	1
16.	1	1	**28.**	1	1
17.	4	1	**29.**	3	1
18.	2	1	**30.**	2	1
19.	1	1	**31.**	2	1
20.	4	1	**32.**	3	1
21.	2	1	**33.**	3	1
22.	3	1	**34.**	1	1
23.	1	2	**35.**	3	1
24.	3	1	**36.**	4	1

PART 2

Question	Number of Points						
	a	**b**	**c**	**d**	**e**	**f**	**g**
1.	1	2	3	4			
2.	1	2	2	2	3	4	
3.	3	1	1	1			
4.	2	3	1	2			
5.	1	1		1			
6.	4	2	1	2	2		
7.	2	1	2	4			
8.	1	1	1	2	3		
9.	1	1	2	3	4		
10.	1	2	4	2	1	1–4	
11.	1	1	1	4	4	4	
12.	2	1	1	3	4		
13.	1	1	1	1	1		
14.	1	1	1	1	1	1	1

Interpreting Your Answers to the Jealousy Diagnostic Index

You'll benefit most from the Jealousy Diagnostic Index by carefully reading this section after you answer the questions. More important than your score are the reasons for answering as you did.

PART 1

1. Everyone knows what jealousy feels like.

You may feel at times as if you're the only one who has known these unpleasant sensations, but in fact everyone has, even people who say they no longer experience jealousy. A recent study showed that 96 percent of people questioned on the subject admitted to feeling jealous within the preceding six months.

In a field test of this question, one young woman hesitated a long while before answering. Later, when asked why she took so long, she said she wondered if the question referred to people of all ages, including children. She couldn't recall whether she'd been jealous as a child. But sibling rivalry usually involves jealousy. Young children not only can accurately describe and define jealousy, they may even feel embarrassed about the emotion just as their elders do. A five-year-old boy once asked me what I was writing about. A book about jealousy, I answered, and then asked him if he knew what jealousy was. "Oh sure," the boy replied, "that's how I feel when my two-year-old brother . . ." He started to describe his feelings, realized what he was saying, then turned the situation around so that his little brother became the jealous party.

2. Sometimes you get so jealous you can't eat.

Loss of appetite is a common response to jealousy. In the film *An Unmarried Woman*, the heroine throws up on learning her husband has decided to seek a divorce. Losing one's appetite might be useful for some people, especially the obese, but not for most of us.

3. Sometimes when you feel jealous, you go on eating binges.

While some people waste away, others have the opposite reaction to jealousy. They start devouring everything in sight, the same response they may have to any emotional crisis. Eating binges often represent a primitive attempt to heal emotional wounds by increasing nutritional intake. But this solution can compound a weighty problem by making us less attractive to others.

4. At parties you are aware of every move and gesture when your partner talks to someone else.

Here is a common situation demonstrating the connection between jealousy, alertness, overalertness, and, perhaps, paranoia. What do those gestures and facial expressions mean? Anything? Nothing? Everything? One of the interview subjects said jealousy caused an intense awareness of his own movements rather than his partner's. This kind of self-consciousness can doom any social event to an ordeal of self-inflicted emotional torture. Few people enjoy this sort of masochism, at least consciously.

5. Jealousy is a major problem in your life.

Although every normal person experiences jealousy at times, it should not, and need not, be a major problem in one's life. If you answered True, at least you recognize that it's a problem. Acknowledging the problem may not be quite like winning half the battle, but it's an important and vital beginning.

6. You are more jealous than most people you know.

If your answer was True, you could really be more jealous than most other people you know or perhaps you're just unaware of their true feelings. Whichever is true, whether you are truly more jealous than most people or only think you are, you can certainly reduce the importance of jealousy in your life. If your answer was False, you're probably correct. Most people have about the same propensity toward jealousy as you do.

7. You should have outgrown jealousy long ago.

Age does seem to give many people experiences that teach them how to cope better with jealousy. But others merely accumulate years and a series of the same bad experiences. Very common is a feeling of shame that the emotion persists as a problem.

What appears as conquest of jealous feelings is, in reality, often a way of masking the truly felt emotions. Most often people grudgingly admit to jealous feelings rather than admitting to them openly and easily. This reaction is only normal. The very nature of jealousy's component parts—grief, anger, shame, loss of a love—precludes feelings cheerful when the emotion is experienced.

This question caused one woman to say, "Well, jealousy keeps people together long enough to have kids." And, in fact, it seems likely that the survival of this emotion is one of the most important reasons for the existence of families, as we have known them.

8. Often you are jealous of your partner's friends even when you know they are not lovers.

Jealousy of nonsexual relationships is an extremely common phenomenon. Although we have been concerned primarily with sexual jealousy, the same dynamics apply to time and attention given other people in nonsexual situations, even to time and attention devoted to things, rather than people. As described in the section on the psychological origins of jealousy, infants don't distinguish at first whether the attention they desire and aren't getting is directed toward other people or toward activities not involving people. They know only that the attention is other-directed.

Jealousy of things may easily be more frustrating than jealousy of another person. One might attempt to compete with another person, but what if the rival is a pack of cards, a job, or a classic automobile?

9. Thinking or hearing about your partner's former lovers makes you jealous.

Most people learn to live comfortably with "ghosts of love past." But the power of jealousy is such that many others become very agitated when reminded of a lover's previous romances, even when they know these relationships ended long ago. Some immature individuals may deliberately invoke the specter of these past loves just to keep their partners "in line," or at a high emotional pitch.

10. Sometimes you seem to like feeling jealous.

Many people do like feeling jealous at times. Their reasons vary. For some, jealousy is an indication they care intensely for another person. Others enjoy the sexual arousal provoked by jealousy (and by other highly charged emotions). Or a person may enjoy the exhilaration of a gripping emotional experience, believing that feeling anything strongly is better than an absence of feeling.

If you frequently enjoy feeling jealousy, you may be "misusing" the emotion, substituting something meant as a warning protective device for your true feelings.

11. Sometimes you like making other people jealous.

Jealousy can be used as a powerful manipulative tool. When one has the option to cause or not cause jealousy, it's sometimes tempting to use this power. But deliberately causing jealousy ultimately hurts everyone involved and is almost always destructive to a relationship.

12. You often like making other people feel jealous.

When children first attempt to manipulate others emotionally, they often experiment with deliberately making people jealous. Eventually children may observe the undesirable consequences of this behavior—notably, the way others tend to avoid them. If as an adult you still enjoy causing jealousy, you likely have serious problems in your relationships. Such behavior is usually a flawed defense against feeling jealous oneself. People who like causing jealousy say to themselves, consciously or unconsciously, "Better to make others jealous than to risk these terrible feelings myself." But the certain result of this behavior is to drive people away. You can learn other and better alternatives.

13. Sometimes you cause jealousy when you don't mean to.

Try as we may, we can't go through life without sometimes causing others to be jealous of us. If you believe you never cause jealousy, you either ignore what sometimes occurs or have very little contact with other people. Though at times we may cause jealousy despite our best intentions, sensitivity to the issue and the feelings of others can greatly reduce the frequency of these incidents.

14. You often seem to cause jealousy when you don't mean to.

Although it's possible you're going through a phase in which rapid change and improvement in certain aspects of your life are causing unavoidable jealousy in others, it's also possible that the jealousy is avoidable and you are either insensitive to what's happening or are "game playing." This is an area where the distinction between jealousy and envy may blur.

15. Jealousy is no longer part of your life.

If even the possibility of jealousy has been eliminated from your life, you are probably putting constraints on your emotions. More likely, you can't or won't admit you're subject to these feelings.

16. You don't care if your partner flirts with others.

Flirtatious behavior by a partner may be significant to a relationship or harmless. Many people flirt at times to assure themselves (and possibly their partners) that they are sexually desirable or otherwise interesting to others. Jealousy may not appear in these cases because the flirtation is infrequent, superficial, and self-limited. Constant flirting is usually a sign of insecurity and immaturity and may not produce jealousy either, when so recognized by a tolerant partner. On the other hand, it is also natural to be annoyed when "made to look bad," as one respondent put it.

17. More than once you have hit a lover or rival because of jealousy.

Jealousy can be so powerful it temporarily deranges a susceptible person. That's why jealous lovers sometimes literally get away with murder—being acquitted or receiving lesser penalties for a "crime of passion." Note, though, that this question stipulates "more than once." To err once is human. "More than once" indicates you haven't benefited from unpleasant experience.

18. More than once you have threatened to hit a lover or rival because of jealousy.

Threats of physical violence neither enhance relationships nor bolster self-esteem. They're either like the snarls of a bluffing animal, soon revealed as so much noise, or worse, a precursor to actual violence.

19. More than once you have thought of hitting a lover or rival because of jealousy.

Everyone has had fantasies that later seem inappropriate, shameful, or unpleasant. But fantasizing differs immeasurably from actual behavior that is inappropriate, shameful, or unpleasant.

20. People seem to go out of their way to make you jealous.

One respondent to this question later asked, "Some people? Which people?" We have probably all, unfortunately, known some people who did go out of their way to cause jealousy. Most of us learn to stay away from such people. A True response to this question could mean that you somehow choose consistently to get involved with those who deliberately induce jealousy.

You might also be inviting this behavior in some way from people who ordinarily don't make a habit of provoking jealousy. It's also possible, maybe likely, that it just *seems* that people go out of their way to cause you jealousy when they're really not. If so, you are being overly suspicious. Let someone help you become more secure again.

21. You have followed or otherwise spied on someone due to jealousy.

Sleuthing is to jealousy as jealousy is to normal behavior. It's almost as common as jealousy itself, a natural extension of the suspicion that breeds, feeds, and accompanies jealousy. Two points are given for a True answer here only because sleuthing almost never turns up anything helpful to a jealous person.

22. Not much time passes between your encounters with jealousy.

While some jealousy is natural and unavoidable, one shouldn't have to be diverted from more useful activities by frequent bouts with it. Whether or not the emotion really besets you more often than it does most people, if it seems that way, you can and should take steps to reduce its power over your thoughts and actions.

23. You are usually successful at controlling your jealous feelings.

Most people believe they can control their jealous feelings or at least disguise them. One respondent to this question said, "True, others can't tell if I'm jealous. I can just not show it if I choose." When asked why she'd choose not to, she replied, "I don't want other people to know. It's just like not burping in public."

Another respondent posed some interesting questions: "What's success in controlling these feelings? Covering them up or expressing them?"

Strong feelings suppressed will eventually leak out or explode if unrelieved. But neither is it socially useful to spill the green-eyed monster's blood uncontrollably in public.

24. You often fly into a jealous rage.

If you are frequently in a rage state due to jealousy—or due to any other reason, for that matter—something is askew in your life. Occasionally expressing the full gamut of emotions is normal and healthy, but to be continuously angry, fearful, or grief-stricken is not useful.

Replying to this question, one middle-aged man grudgingly admitted he lost his "cool" when he thought his partner lied to him. Deceit or suspected deceit is especially disturbing to someone inclined toward jealousy, since that person likely tends to be overalert.

25. When you're jealous, it's hard to admit it to others.

Since jealousy is so often associated with guilt and shame, it's not surprising people find it hard to admit their feelings to others or even to themselves. Yet confessing one's troubled thoughts to another person is a time-tested, valuable means of relief. Several interviewees who had undergone some form of psychotherapy commented that dealing with jealousy became easier for them after they relearned to express their innermost feelings.

26. At social functions like parties you tend to stay very close to your partner to fend off possible rivals.

What's the point of going to social functions if you spend your time hovering over your partner to fend off possible rivals? Even more to the point, as a lawyer friend said about her experiences, "Chances are, the more you hover, the more the other person will feel confined and want to go away." However, you may want to reevaluate your social activities while working out this particular problem.

27. You must know where your partner is at all times.

Although modern technology makes it literally possible to know where a partner is at all times (see the "beeper" incident in Chapter 2, The Jealousy Follies), insisting on this knowledge indicates, to say the least, a lack of trust. You probably have more productive things to do than continually monitoring your partner's whereabouts.

28. You have fantasized about taking revenge on a rival.

Most people have at some point thought about wreaking revenge on a rival. These thoughts are common and normal. The fantasies range from ghastly scenarios of mayhem to pie-in-the-face plans. One woman's idea of appropriate vengeance was stomping on her rival's toe with a spiked heel. "It would feel great," she said. Occasional fantasies of this type are harmless. Carrying them out may cause irreparable harm to all concerned.

Perhaps you've never really fantasized about taking revenge on a rival. If so, you seem to be in the minority or are fooling yourself. We'll give you the benefit of the doubt.

29. You have taken revenge on a rival.

We usually absolve the loved one of blame in these matters and go after the rival instead. It's only natural in a way. Why hurt and drive away the one we love? Easier to pin it all on someone else, after all.

While "all's fair in love" usually refers to the courting period before engagement or marriage, a true threat to an established relationship necessarily involves the willing cooperation of the loved one. Blaming the rival is illogical, if understandable.

A respondent to this question said her revenge consisted of thoroughly and accurately delineating to her ex-lover all the faults of her rival. While revenge may seem quite satisfying at the time, it seldom restores a loved one to the hearth in the absence of other measures.

30. Jealousy has caused you to consider hiring a private detective.

Since "sleuthing" is such a common phenomenon, it's not surprising so many people consider hiring a professional to do the job. Only the expense and unfamiliarity with detective-hiring practices stop many from carrying through this idea.

The thought of hiring a private eye has crossed so many jealous minds it's reasonable to question whether a False answer to this question is a false answer and should receive 1 or 4 points. But we'll again give the benefit of a doubt.

31. You tell people you're not the jealous type, even though you may be very jealous indeed.

Since jealousy currently has such a bad reputation, it's not surprising if you don't like to face up to it. That's why you get only 2 points for a True response.

While there's no use groveling in jealous self-pity, admitting to jealous feelings is the first step to dealing with irrational jealousy.

32. You avoid close relationships because such situations can lead to jealousy.

The best use of this or any other test is learning from the questions, not the final score. Jealousy is so traumatic to many people that they'd rather avoid close relationships than be burdened with negative feelings. Rather than risk the peaks and valleys of romantic love, they keep their emotional distance.

If you answered False, your theory seems to be "Better to have loved and risked jealousy than never to have loved at all."

33. It would be a major crisis if you discovered your partner had had a casual sexual encounter with someone else.

According to all studies of the issue, monogamy throughout a relationship is an endangered species. Therefore, lamentable as it may be, a casual sexual encounter by your partner should not threaten the entire relationship. Jealousy in these circumstances, though, is normal and to be expected.

Since we're dealing with individual standards of behavior and morality here, it's difficult to fairly assign a point value to this question. If this question were asked of an Algerian living in a small village, a False response would be an aberration.

34. It would be a major crisis if you discovered a continuing, though casual, sexual relationship.

Although a long-standing but newly discovered casual sexual relationship need not endanger a primary relationship, at least in the sense of breaking it up, it certainly can and usually does provoke jealousy. In this situation, jealousy is normal.

If your partner has a continuing sexual relationship with someone else and it doesn't bother you, fine. But if that other relationship really does threaten yours, then it's not fine. In that case, jealousy is in order if you care for your partner and the relationship. One respondent commented that the situation posed by the question would give her a feeling of "taking away from what I've got." Others might not be disturbed by a partner's outside sexual activities.

35. You find it hard to accept criticism.

If it's difficult for you to accept criticism, you may also be subject to inordinate jealousy. The connection is that sensitivity to criticism indicates either temporary or deep-seated feelings of insecurity. In this state a person is more prone to bouts of jealousy.

If you can accept criticism with grace, you likely have better access to the inner reserves of self-esteem possessed by everyone.

36. You are generally pretty lonely.

Being lonely is not the same as being alone. Existentialists like philosopher Jean-Paul Sartre and psychologist Rollo May point out that we are basically alone, in a sense truly apart from all others. But that's not the same as being lonely. All of us at times have felt lonely, perhaps even when among large numbers of other people. If you feel lonely much of the time, you likely tend toward problems with jealousy. The reason? When you do become emotionally attached to someone else and you feel less lonely, the threat of losing that person seems all the more significant.

Taking steps to make yourself less lonely will therefore have the benefit of making you less prone to jealousy.

PART 2

1. A person with whom you're nonexclusively involved receives a telephone call while the two of you are watching TV. Judging from the conversation and tone of voice, the caller is also involved with your partner. The conversation lasts a friendly five minutes. You would feel:

a. Unconcerned

Being unconcerned in this situation is normal. You weren't engaged in conversation with this person, just watching television with someone who you know has other relationships.

b. Mildly irritated

Many people would feel mildly irritated, though it is not justified. But then jealousy is so frequently illogical.

c. Offended and resentful

In answering these questions, you probably refer back to situations from your own life. Either you want more of a relationship with your fellow TV viewer, or you are too susceptible to jealousy.

d. Really angry

You need to work on your jealousy soon, before it disrupts your relationship. One woman said that this situation could make her angry because she'd be a captive audience, "although I could always get up and go to the refrigerator or something." What length conversation would you think proper? Three minutes? Two minutes? Sometimes these small details mean the difference (temporarily) between tranquillity and angry outbursts. When dealing with the jealousy of others, it may be wise to attend to such details.

2. In the preceding situation, you would:

a. Dismiss the episode as unimportant

The episode, as described (an actual incident), was really unimportant.

b. Ask who the caller was, though you're not jealous

A friend who took this quiz said she might just be curious about the caller even if she wasn't jealous. But even if you're not jealous, it's not really your business who called.

c. Ask who the caller was because you're feeling jealous

Well, at least you know your feelings.

d. Hide your feelings and hope they'll pass in a while

Maybe it's better not to make a scene and your feelings will pass. But don't ignore this signal. For some reason, you do feel jealous.

e. Tell your partner the caller should have been asked to call back at another time

You're out of line and may soon be out of the house as well.

f. Get up and leave the house

Ending communication with this dramatic gesture helps nothing.

- 3. You've just returned from a week-long business trip. You and your live-in partner pay a visit to a mutual friend next door. At one point your neighbor is looking for an appointment book. "Isn't it in the top drawer of your bedroom dresser?" your partner asks helpfully. You would:

a. Think nothing of the remark

Think nothing of the remark? Whether or not you care about your partner's other relationships, you've been alerted to something going on here. It's been suggested, by a woman, that an exception might be two women who spend time in each other's bedrooms socially, but not sexually.

b. Suspect some hanky-panky

Given the situation, it would be natural to suspect something might have occurred in your absence.

c. Suspect hanky-panky and be jealous

The remark was unusual so it's natural to wonder how it originated.

d. Consider other reasons for your partner's remark

You're secure, on top of things, and on to something. It's possible there was no hanky-panky, isn't it? In the real situation where this question originated, no physical "infidelity" had really taken place.

4. In these circumstances, you would:

a. Say nothing

Whether you're unconcerned or not, your partner said something bound to provoke you. You shouldn't just let this pass without question or comment of some kind.

b. Do nothing for the time being, but be watchful

Once those fires of jealousy rise, it's hard to put them out. Sleuthing will only make you feel worse. Better to resolve the issue right away.

c. Ask for an explanation when you're alone with your partner if the matter concerns you

Naturally, your partner expects some kind of reaction, so why not give it? Not in the face though. Just ask what's going on.

d. Confront both of them right then and get to the bottom of it.

Your neighbor might be innocent of any mischief. There's something to be said for quick resolution of problems. In fact, when this situation did occur, the neighbor was innocent. The traveler's partner deliberately tried to make him jealous. She'd once observed her neighbor put his appointment book in a dresser drawer during a party. So don't jump to hasty conclusions. But do listen.

5. You learn your supposedly monogamous partner has another lover. You would feel:

a. Annoyed

Whatever the merits of making rules in a relationship, you and your partner have done so and there's been a transgression. You've got a right to be annoyed.

b. Relieved

Some people really do wish their partners had other lovers. As one New York attorney put it, "I only wish he had another lover." Some people feel their partners are sexual burdens and want others to share the responsibility—even though they don't wish to disrupt the total relationship. Or they may wish to relieve guilt over their own affairs.

c. Somewhat jealous

In this situation it's certainly normal to be jealous. The extent of jealousy depends on how you feel about your partner, the relationship, and, most important, yourself.

d. Betrayed, angry, and hurt

It's also normal to feel betrayed, angry, and hurt when your partner deceives you in this fashion.

6. Accordingly, you would:

a. Say nothing; hide your feelings

If you say nothing and try to hide your feelings, the pent-up emotions will only surface another time, perhaps inappropriately.

b. Do nothing as long as your partner continues to give you the same amount of warmth and affection

You should do something, even if it's only self-evaluation, because a change has developed in your relationship.

c. Confront your partner, express your feelings, and work through the crisis

By dealing with the situation rather than ignoring it, you'll relieve yourself and possibly your partner as well.

d. Plan your revenge

Although Jack Margolis, a former author turned Los Angeles real-estate mogul, claims revenge is one of life's vital necessities, and you can undoubtedly concoct plots of delicious retribution, your time is much better spent improving yourself and your relationships.

e. Finding another lover for yourself

This is one possible solution, but not the best.

7. You are invited to an important dinner party where a serious rival for your partner will also be a guest. You would feel:

a. No jealousy

Feeling no jealousy in this situation means you are supremely self-confident, don't care that much for your partner, or are out of touch with your feelings. If it's the first give yourself only 1 point for this answer.

b. A little jealous

Sure, it's normal to feel a bit jealous in this situation. There's a serious rival for your honey.

c. Jealous and jittery

Why are you jittery? Is there really a chance for your rival? In any case, being jittery won't help, so try to do something to calm your nerves and your fears.

d. Very jealous—enraged, fear-stricken

You'd best acknowledge to yourself you've got a bit of a problem involving jealousy.

8. You would then:

a. Accept the invitation; the guest list gives you no problem

Okay, we're still assuming you're very confident of yourself, your partner, and the relationship. However, jealousy functions, in part, as a warning of danger. You might blunder into a situation and come out minus a partner. Of course, if you are so confident, you may not be much concerned anyway. You'll also know that, just as two people well matched might as well stay together because they won't be any happier with other partners, it's also the case that the idea that there's only one true love for each of us seems to be a fallacy.

b. Discuss your feelings with your partner before accepting the invitation

Discussing your feelings is generally a good idea, but this course of action does hold some danger. A lover's jealousy often seems flattering—that's why some people actually provoke jealousy in others. There's also a possibility of arousing more interest in the rival than previously existed.

c. Accept the invitation, then discuss your feelings with your partner

Accepting the invitation, then discussing your feelings, indicates to your partner that you are in control of the situation and in touch with your feelings.

d. Decline the invitation without admitting the reason

One problem with this answer is the obvious limits placed on sociability. A policy of avoiding potential rivals may leave you spending a lot of time looking at the same four walls.

e. Declare your feelings and decline the invitation

Declining the invitation this way indicates you fear the rival and fail to let your partner share decisions. Your partner may resent your heavy-handed approach and wonder if your fears are justified.

9. You accepted the invitation. On the way home your partner is bubbling with happiness. You would feel:

a. Curious

It's only natural to be curious about what made your partner so happy.

b. Pleased your partner had a good time

In the best of all possible emotional worlds, you should be happy when your partner has a good time.

c. A little jealous for a little while

When you feel deprived of your partner's attention or threatened by your partner's attention to someone else, it's not unusual to be a bit jealous.

d. Very jealous and angry

Was there really enough provocation to feel really jealous? Are you being overalert?

e. Like punching out your partner or the other person

Whoa! You're in danger of losing your partner and your freedom, as well as your temper.

10. Once home, your partner wants to make love. You feel jealous. You would:

a. Make love, if you felt like it

Making love with a happy person spreads happiness

b. Hide your jealous feelings and make love

Hiding or trying to hide your feelings is seldom a good idea. In this case, you may be distracted from good lovemaking.

c. Invent a "headache" type excuse

Sometimes people just don't feel like making love and that's fine. But when you know the reason and make up an excuse instead of revealing your feelings, that's not fine at all.

d. Vent your feelings and declare you don't want to make love

Try not to be fixed in your ideas or plans. Venting your feelings is a good idea. Threats aren't.

e. Vent your feelings, then see what happens

Chances are, venting your feelings here would lead to a passionate love scene. Talking about jealousy often turns people on sexually.

f. Make passionate love to get your partner very interested in you

This answer was almost discarded with an earlier draft, but it was read inadvertently to a woman physician who declared that, yes, she would attempt passionate lovemaking to get back her partner's attention. Of course, jealousy itself creates passion. And an attempt at passion may turn to passion anyway. Give yourself 1 to 4 points depending on how well you've succeeded in the past. Anyway, it's better than pouting.

11. Since arriving at another party, your partner has been totally engrossed in conversation with someone else. You would:

a. Be unconcerned

Nothing wrong with being unconcerned here. Your partner could have many reasons for being so thoroughly engaged in conversation.

b. Ignore the situation for now, but discuss it later when the two of you are alone

If you're concerned, there's nothing wrong with discussing your feelings. But you might reflect first on whether there's even a reason to discuss the matter, unless you felt your partner was rude or embarrassed either of you in some manner.

c. Take your partner aside and calmly express your feelings

If you're uncomfortable because your partner has spent no time with you, it probably does no harm to talk it over briefly, privately, and calmly.

d. Tell your partner you're leaving unless more attention is paid to you

Maybe your partner is misbehaving, maybe not. Either way, nothing is gained by threats.

e. Leave the party and drive home alone

Leaving the party in this matter helps nothing. People who react like this may salvage their pride but lose the object of their affection.

f. Leave the party with a different partner

Unless you're ready right now to trade your partner for the one you've just picked up, this is the wrong move.

12. Your partner is quite vulnerable to jealousy but at the moment is openly flirting with someone else. You feel jealous. You would:

a. Try to ignore the situation

Trying to ignore jealousy is virtually hopeless. It's a strong, basic emotion and meant to be that way.

b. Take your partner aside privately and explain how you feel

That's right, you feel uncomfortable. Try to rectify the situation, but don't embarrass or humiliate yourself or your partner.

c. Do nothing until the party is over, then discuss your feelings

No use interrupting a social gathering, but don't ignore your feelings either.

d. Tell your partner right now to stop flirting

Some people like to be ordered about, but mature people don't, even when they are acting immaturely. Giving an order this way is likely to cause resentment rather than understanding.

e. Find someone you can flirt with too

Flirting in order to retaliate against a partner doing the same is also immature as well as unproductive.

13. You discover your partner is involved in a homosexual relationship. You would feel:

a. No jealousy

A male author whose wife has extramarital relationships with both men and women says the lesbian relationships cause him no jealousy, but her affairs with other men do. I'd say he was a sexist.

b. Jealous, but less so than if it was a heterosexual relationship

One reason this situation may produce less jealousy is the lack of a sense of permanent loss. Most people don't fear their mates will completely exchange their relationships for that with someone of the same sex. Sometimes they're wrong.

c. More jealous than if it was a heterosexual relationship

One woman responding to this question said, "I wouldn't know how to compete. I can gain weight, lose weight, or curl my hair. But I can't grow a penis." And presumably wouldn't consider surgery.

d. Equally jealous regardless of the rival's sex

This seems a normal nonsexist response.

e. Perplexed

Being perplexed seems the most common initial response when someone finds a partner involved in a homosexual relationship. Some people would not feel threatened, others more so than by a same-sex rival. One woman said her feelings would depend on whether the situation was experimental.

14. You have a close relationship with someone, but both of you have sex with others and know it. The proper time interval your partner should observe between sex with others and with you is:

a. The time interval doesn't matter

Most people don't wish to rush in where others have recently tread. But some people say, in theory, anyway, "It doesn't matter."

b. The time interval doesn't matter as long as you don't know about it

Many people operate under this theory. They know their partners have other relationships and can deal successfully with this fact if they are not confronted with it directly.

c. A week or more

Desire and jealousy are more closely related to each other than they are to logic and good intentions. Desire, like jealousy, has a way of altering one's idea of what constitutes good behavior. A recently divorced woman responded, "Part of me says a week, but what if we just wanted to do it?"

d. Several days

Most respondents to this question believe "several days" would be appropriate in this situation. One young woman asked a very practical question: "How long does it take for gonorrhea to appear?" (One to nine days on average.)

e. One day

Even a film director whose philosophy of multiple relationships was "It doesn't matter if you don't know about it" gave this response. She wanted at least a day's distance.

f. A few hours with a shower and/or douche

Few wish the scent or cells of another, on or in the body of a lover.

g. One hour with a Boraxo-soap shower and/or industrial-strength douche

This last answer is for laughs, but the overall question seemed to cause the most difficulty for a test group taking the Jealousy Diagnostic Index.